SKIM

D.P. DART

SKIM

*Dedicated to my grandsons, Bishop and Jackson, and—as always—
to my wife for her support.
Special thanks to Carolyn Simi, my sole beta reader.*

CONTENTS

CHAPTER 1
ROOKIE

The terminal pinged.

It was a soft sound, barely audible over the steady hum of the AS/400 machines, but to Matt Hall it might as well have been applause. He leaned back in his chair, cracked his knuckles, and exhaled a breath he hadn't realized he'd been holding. Four weeks of grinding out COBOL routines, late-night syntax checks, and debugging by flashlight in the back corner of the server room—finally finished.

Martin, his boss, hadn't expected him to hit the deadline for another two weeks. Honestly, Matt hadn't either. The spec sheet for the overnight reporting module had looked daunting, but once the puzzle clicked in his brain, he didn't want to stop. He found the process intoxicating: the logic, the structure, the lines of code being coaxed into precision. It was like threading order through chaos, pulling steel wire through the eye of a needle, or completing a complex puzzle.

"Done?"

The voice came from behind him. British accent. Clipped, curious. Martin Jepson.

Matt turned. "Yup. Pushed the build to test a few minutes ago."

Martin raised an eyebrow and stepped forward, arms crossed over his navy blazer. He looked more like a professor than a banker: lean, slightly disheveled, with steel-gray hair that never quite obeyed a comb.

"Four weeks. That was quick."

Matt shrugged, aiming for casual. "I just sort of—well, got into a rhythm."

Martin scrolled through the commit logs, then opened the build report. The silence stretched. Finally: *No errors.*

Matt tried to suppress his grin. "Clean compile. First time."

Now Martin looked at him differently, not as a manager looks at a summer intern, but as a craftsman regards a new tool he hadn't expected to like.

"In 30 years," he said slowly, "I've never seen a first push that bloody clean."

Matt's grin escaped. "Guess I got lucky."

"Luck had nothing to do with it." Martin tapped the monitor, then turned to him. "We need to talk about post-graduation."

A year earlier, Matt hadn't even known what COBOL was.

He'd left his Brooklyn high school for UConn in August 1992 with two duffel bags, a partial swim scholarship, and a pit in his stomach. The late summer heat clung to the city like damp laundry, and the platform at Flatbush Avenue station smelled of oil. His parents had done their best to hide their anxiety, but he knew the truth: college was a financial stretch. Between grants, aid packages, student loans he'd signed half-blind, and the money he'd scraped together fixing PCs around the neighborhood, they were still short. And there was nothing to fall back on.

His dad, who drove the 2 line for the MTA, had suggested trade school: electrician, plumber, honest work. His mom, exhausted after long shifts at Walmart, just wanted him safe.

"No debt," she'd said. "No risk."

Matt's neighborhood didn't produce many college kids. Most of the boys he grew up with either joined the service, found union jobs, or stayed close to home. Going away to university, let alone studying something as abstract as computer science, felt like fantasy. Cracked sidewalks lined their block, fire escapes rattled in the wind, and cars with rusted-out fenders coughed down the street. The corner store smelled of cigarettes. Vacations meant a paper plate of fries at Coney Island. Ambition meant overtime.

But Matt was different. Not smarter necessarily, just wired to see patterns where others didn't. When he was a kid, he took apart the family VCR to see if he could put it back together. By 16, he was making pocket money resurrecting old dinosaur computers for neighbors. He loved it.

School was the one place where he received praise without having to hustle for it. But it wasn't easy. He'd swim before sunrise in a pool that smelled of chlorine, sit through classes half asleep, then come home to help with chores or bag groceries under flickering fluorescent lights. When he finally sat down at a keyboard, it felt like stepping into another world, one where rules made sense, and outcomes were fair.

His first year at UConn was rough. Balancing swim meets with late-night science labs nearly broke him. He scraped by, just barely. But in the spring, while learning how to build a basic database for a small software application, something clicked. He began to love it. Not the lectures or the grades, but the feeling of making things work, solving problems with logic and elegance. Application development, they called it. He called it magic.

By his second year, things had stabilized. He was still on the swim team but had accepted the truth: he wasn't Olympic material. His future wasn't in the water. It was in a data center or even a lab, where the hum of servers and the glow of monochrome screens felt more like home than any locker room.

The summer before his second year, after a dozen ignored internship applications, he got a call from Camden Bank. A guy named Martin Jepson was on the line.

"I'm told you know your way around a mainframe," Martin had said. "Ever touched COBOL?"

Matt hadn't, but he said *yes*. Then he crammed for 72 hours before day one.

He showed up at 277 Park Avenue in a borrowed shirt and tie, shoes a half-size too big, found the server room, and met Martin in person: a British technologist with the manners of a schoolmaster and the brain of an engineer. Martin was building something new: a tool called PulseFX that would help traders price FX forward positions with greater accuracy than any other bank had achieved.

"It's a beast," Martin said, showing him the architecture diagram. "Front end is C. Back end's AS/400, all COBOL. We need it bulletproof."

Matt dove in. He spent the next two summers coding for PulseFX, writing modules, testing legacy routines, optimizing batch processes. Cables snaked under metal tiles while fans whirred like background radiation. Martin pushed him hard, expected results, but also gave him freedom.

It was the first place Matt felt as if he actually mattered.

And now, by the early spring of '94, just before graduation, he'd delivered more than just code. He'd delivered trust.

Martin was still at the terminal.

"I meant what I said," he told Matt. "After you graduate, we'd like you back. Full time."

Matt nodded, heart pounding. "I'd like that."

Martin gave a slight smile. "Don't go getting any better offers."

Matt laughed, but part of him already knew this was only the beginning.

He still had a lot more building to do.

CHAPTER 2
MENTOR

M att hadn't expected the end of university to arrive so quickly. One moment, he was grinding out problem sets and pulling all-nighters in the computer lab. The next, he was standing under a flurry of confetti in the UConn gymnasium, grinning as his name rang out over the loudspeaker.

Matthew Hall. Bachelor of Science, Computer Science.

His parents were in the bleachers, waving wildly, his mother dabbing her eyes with a tissue she'd clutched since the ceremony began. They had never been prouder.

Matt was the first person on either side of his parents' family to graduate from college.

Outside, in the dewy May air, cameras flashed. Caps spun skyward. The knot in Matt's chest refused to loosen.

Matt's girlfriend, Bernice, stood beside him, radiant in a pale yellow sundress that danced in the breeze. She pinned her blonde hair back in soft waves, pearl earrings catching the light. She looked as if she'd stepped out of a southern bridal magazine, but behind the smile was something else—an ache, a shadow.

The couple had at most three months left together. They both knew it.

Bernice, who was five months younger than Matt, was from Marietta, Georgia, a place that felt impossibly far from Brooklyn in every sense. Her childhood home had white shutters, a porch swing, and a mailbox shaped like a golden retriever. Her parents believed in manners, college football, and linen napkins. She had been their only child, the belle of every school event and the star of every church fundraiser.

They had met freshman year through the swim team, but it wasn't until the end-of-year athletic banquet that things changed. A glance. A laugh. An awkward, tipsy dance. That was all it took.

In the weeks leading up to graduation, Matt had lived in a fog of excitement and dread. He'd reached out to Martin Jepson in April to confirm the job offer still stood. The reply came back instantly: Of course, and I look forward to it. Two days later, a formal letter arrived.

Junior Developer, starting September 15, 1994. Salary: $60,000.

Matt stared at the number for a long time. It was more than double what his father made driving the 2 line.

But the money didn't ease the ache in his gut when he looked at Bernice.

They told themselves it wasn't goodbye. Bernice applied for jobs in New York. Matt promised to visit Atlanta. They discussed finding an apartment together, somewhere new, somewhere that would be theirs. Behind every plan, though, was a ticking clock.

A week after graduation, Matt booked a cheap flight to Atlanta. He didn't tell anyone but Bernice. They spent the weekend in a boutique hotel near Piedmont Park, charm over budget, her style as always. She arrived with a floral overnight bag, a silk scarf tied in her hair, and a tote full of Southern Living magazines. For a few days, they lived inside their own bubble: sweet tea from room service, early-morning cartoons, and shared showers.

One evening, as they watched the sunset from the balcony, she said, "Mama's still not sure about you. She thinks you don't say 'sir' or 'ma'am' enough. But don't worry. You make me happy. And that's something even she can't ignore."

On their last night, she traced a finger along his jaw and asked, half-laughing, "Do you think you'll still call me in a month?"

"Every day," he said.

And he meant it.

NOT LONG AFTER, Matt walked through the marble lobby of 277 Park Avenue for his first day as a junior developer at Camden Bank; the place smelled of fresh paint and money. He wore a stiff new suit that itched around the collar, and his shoes were stiff and tight, still not broken in. After orientation, they sent him to Martin's office, a glass-fronted corner space overlooking the chaos of the trading floor.

PulseFX had been a triumph. The traders loved it, and Martin had been promoted to global head of trading applications. He greeted Matt with a firm handshake and a brief, almost imperceptible smile. Then he directed him two floors down.

Matt's new office was a world away from Martin's perch. A windowless room housing five other developers, humming with CRT monitors. He was part of a three-person team tasked with building a real-time auto-reconciliation tool to help traders manage their positions. It was unglamorous work, but essential, and the code they developed had to be fast, resilient, and invisible until it failed.

The hours were brutal. Most nights, he didn't leave before nine, and sometimes not at all. The traders barked like drill sergeants, speaking in acronyms, demanding results *yesterday*.

But Matt didn't mind; he was 22, writing production code for one of the world's largest banks. The systems he touched moved billions. The pressure was immense, but so was the rush. He was in his element.

And he loved the money. Still living at home, he contributed to his parents' household expenses and saved aggressively, to the point of near obsession—his way of building armor.

At home, however, the cracks were evident. The distance between him and Bernice wasn't just geography anymore; it was emotional.

He still called her, but the conversations had changed. What used to be laughter and longing had turned into silence and sighs. She asked about his day; he gave clipped answers, already thinking about tomorrow's bug list. She shared news about friends or interviews, while he only half-listened.

He missed her perfume on his pillow, her habit of folding dresses over padded hangers like heirlooms, but it all felt like a postcard now. Beautiful, distant, trapped behind glass.

She wanted more of him.

He didn't know how to give it.

One Thursday night in late January, Martin invited him out for drinks.

They walked to a narrow, wood-paneled bar on Lexington called Marcos, "a holdover from the days when men wore hats." Martin's go-to bar. They slid into a booth and ordered pints.

"You're doing bloody good work," Martin said after a sip.

"Trying to keep up," Matt responded.

Martin smiled faintly. "Bonus season's coming. I've already put your name forward. I will make sure you are taken care of."

Matt blinked. "Really?"

"I'm recommending 25."

Matt nearly choked. "Thousand?"

"It's more than most first-years get. But you're not most."

Matt sat back, stunned. His mind raced. Twenty-five thousand. He imagined handing his mother an envelope stuffed with bills, replacing the ones marked *Rent*, *Groceries*, and *Emergency*, all kept in a hidden shoebox. Or taking his dad to buy a car that wasn't rusting through and ending his mother's need to check every price tag meticulously. Maybe even putting down the first month's rent on a place of his own—with Bernice, if they could figure it out. They could have proper furniture that wasn't secondhand and go to restaurants where the menus didn't come laminated.

It wasn't greed. It was relief.

He nodded slowly. "Thank you."

"You earned it," Martin said. "Just keep going."

They clinked glasses. Matt couldn't stop smiling.

TWO WEEKS LATER, Matt was in a development meeting with Martin and the rest of the team. The air was dry and still, monitors humming, as everyone squinted at spaghetti diagrams on the whiteboard.

Martin was mid-sentence when he stopped abruptly. His hand went to his chest. His brow furrowed. Then he collapsed.

The room erupted. Chairs scraped. Someone shouted. Matt froze for a heartbeat, then dropped to his side. Someone was already calling 911. Martin's lips had gone pale, his eyes open but glassy.

The EMTs arrived in under 10 minutes. Everything became blurred—flashing lights, the stretcher, Martin being wheeled through double doors and swallowed by the elevators.

Matt jumped into a taxi and followed the ambulance to the hospital. A nauseating antiseptic smell hovered in the waiting room, mixing with the scent of coffee. Fluorescent lights buzzed overhead, washing everything in a sickly yellow. Time stuttered: minutes dragged on, then hours slipped away.

A nurse finally called for the Jepson family. Matt saw them —a woman in her early 40s, tear-streaked, dazed, with two children huddled close, one in a Yankees cap. She glanced at Matt, her eyes red, her mouth tight, conveying a silent *thank you*. He didn't approach, only nodded and sat back down.

Half an hour later, a doctor confirmed what HR would later announce officially: cardiac arrest. No warning. He was gone.

Back at the office, Matt sat alone long after everyone else had left. The terminals dimmed, the server fans still whirred, but the room felt hollow. The man who had pulled him from obscurity, who had taught him how to thrive, was gone.

For the first time since starting at Camden, the confidence that had carried him through long nights and tight deadlines gave way to something new: doubt. The architecture diagrams pinned to the wall looked meaningless. Martin had been more than a boss. He had been a compass. Now, with that compass gone, Matt felt untethered, adrift in a place that once gave him purpose. Now, it was just another floor of blinking lights and empty chairs.

Later that night, lying in bed, his eyes drifted to a Polaroid Bernice had given him before he left Atlanta. She was in that same yellow sundress, blowing him a kiss with one hand, holding a peach in the other. On the back, in looping cursive, she had written: *Don't forget what sweet tastes like.*

He hadn't. Not yet.

CHAPTER 3
FLIGHT

The funeral had barely ended when the fog set in. Matt went back to work, but something fundamental had shifted. The vibrant thrum of the trading floor rang hollow. Martin was gone. The systems still ran, deadlines still loomed, yet the heartbeat had stopped. Every flicker of a screen, every keystroke, felt mechanical.

The bank moved fast. Within a week, the company named Stephen Walker as head of trading applications. Matt recognized him from hallways and elevators, a background figure, all hard edge and policy. There was no welcome, no handshake, just a sterile memo and a change in weather.

Stephen treated Matt like an afterthought. The collaborative whiteboard sessions vanished. In their place came curt directives, point-scored code reviews, and a tone that made Matt feel like an intern fetching coffee. Months earlier, he'd been writing mission-critical modules; now he was working on low-level fault tickets for loud traders. The dream job turned into a joyless march.

The first actual clash came when Matt identified a bug in one of the core reconciliation modules.

Martin had trusted him to resolve these issues directly, often giving him latitude to rework the codebase.

This time, however, Stephen shut him down in the middle of a meeting.

"Document it and assign it to the main development group," he said flatly, not even looking up from his notes. "Stay in your lane."

The words stung. A colleague caught Matt's eye with an apologetic shrug, but no one spoke up. The message was clear: Matt's ideas weren't welcome anymore.

A week later, Stephen reassigned Matt from the new-feature-rollout group to old-batch-job maintenance, work that no one wanted. Matt sat through a meeting in which Stephen praised another developer for implementing a change Matt had suggested months earlier without acknowledgment. When Matt tried to raise his concern, Stephen cut him off with a clipped, "Not now, Hall."

The humiliation deepened when Stephen began reviewing Matt's coding jobs in front of the team. What Martin had treated as teaching moments, Stephen weaponized.

"This is sloppy," he said one morning, circling Matt's code on a projected screen. "We don't have time for shortcuts."

Matt knew the code was clean; the problem had been in upstream data feeds. But Stephen never let him explain. The silence of the room pressed down on him, and for the first time, Matt doubted himself.

One night at home, his parents watched as he pushed his dinner around on his plate, showing no interest in eating. He continued sitting at the table after the dishes were cleared, silently spinning his fork. His mother went into worrying mode; his father tried quiet encouragement. Neither could reach him. On weekends, he wandered the neighborhood out of habit, past the corner store with its pungent smell of fried grease, past the subway entrance where his father disappeared each morning. But it was all distant; he felt like a ghost in his own city.

One Wednesday evening, his mother sat beside him and said gently, "Go see Bernice, sweetheart." She was right.

That weekend, he flew to Atlanta. Bernice met him at the airport and wrapped herself around him as if she meant to keep him from breaking. She wore a navy sundress touched with small, embroidered flowers; her hair was tied back with a silk ribbon. "Took you long enough," she whispered, eyes bright.

They checked into a quiet hotel and pretended the outside world didn't exist. They wandered through Piedmont Park hand in hand, ate greasy takeout in bed, talked until the room dimmed to the blue of the TV. She had just started as a junior accountant with the Atlanta United soccer team and spoke with quick energy about streamlining expense tracking and taming vendor reconciliations. Matt didn't follow every detail, but he loved the spark in her voice. Later, she teased him for ordering pizza instead of trying the new Cuban place around the corner, then kissed the grease from his lips. For a night, life was light again.

That night, with her head on his chest, she asked, "Do you think this is where we're supposed to end up? Here? You and me?"

He hesitated, not from doubt, but from how much he wanted it. "Yeah," he said. "I do."

For a moment, the fog lifted. He laughed with his entire face for the first time in months.

Flying back to New York on Sunday, he stared out the window with something like clarity. By Tuesday, the gray had crept back in. The office was as joyless as before. Stephen was even sharper. Martin's absence felt like an elusive draft in an old house. Even casual conversations with coworkers turned clipped; the camaraderie had drained away.

Back in the office, the breaking point came during a Friday meeting. Stephen presented a new architecture diagram, one Matt had helped design with Martin months earlier. Without a word of credit, Stephen dismissed the original approach as "naïve" and credited his own adjustments. Matt opened his mouth to speak, but stopped when Stephen's eyes cut across the table, daring him. The room fell silent. Rage tightened Matt's chest, but he swallowed it down. The truth was obvious: Martin's trust had died with him, and Stephen would never give Matt a place at the table.

That night, staring at a water stain on the ceiling, Matt decided: he couldn't do it anymore. He needed to leave Camden Bank, leave New York, and move nearer to Bernice.

In the days that followed, he plunged into finding a job in Atlanta—résumés, calls to old professors, measured conversations with strangers. Most leads evaporated. He found himself writing cover letters at 2 a.m. while his parents slept in the next room, the glow of his monitor the only light in the kitchen.

Then came Ira Rosenburg.

Ira ran a one-man recruiting shop in upstate New York. Raspy voice, dry wit, the patience of a saint. He listened to what Matt wanted, but more importantly, he heard *why* Matt wanted what he did. Ira told stories about the industry, about deals that had collapsed because of hubris or systems that had ruined careers. He laughed easily but took Matt seriously. By some miracle, he'd just come across the search for a COBOL developer with financial services experience. The client was Sunbelt Business Funding, or SBF, in Kennesaw, Georgia—not far from Marietta. Matt had never heard of it, and when Ira explained the business, it sounded like an illegal lending operation.

"Feels like fate, doesn't it?" Ira said.

After a few calls, Ira lined up a phone screen with SBF's head of HR, Debbie How: blunt, friendly, allergic to fluff.

"You know your way around an AS/400?"

"Like the back of my hand," Matt said.

Two weeks later, he flew to Georgia for interviews.

He built the trip around a night with Bernice. Her apartment smelled faintly of vanilla. She'd lit candles, set out a bowl of fruit, and chilled a bottle of sweet white wine. Barefoot, hair up, cotton dress. She tucked her legs across his lap and asked about every detail of his prep.

"They're going to love you," she said. "Just don't let 'em lowball you."

They argued playfully about whether New York bagels really were better, then fell asleep tangled on her sofa with the candles burning low.

The next morning, Matt headed to SBF's modest office: a low brick and glass facade beside a credit union and a barbecue place that smelled of smoked oak and brown sugar. The inside: quiet purpose.

Matt met Debbie, then Rajive Singh, head of application development—sharp, thorough, and no-nonsense. After that, Richard Eastern, the CTO. Finally, Dennis Robinson, the CEO, with the easy polish of a man who knew the cost of every decision.

They pushed hard and listened harder. Rajive quizzed him on batch processing, Dennis pressed on long-term goals, and Richard asked about mistakes and how he handled them. When Matt stepped back into the Georgia sun, he felt something he hadn't felt in a long time: possibility.

He flew to New York that night, arrived home after midnight, and called Bernice. For an hour, they planned their future as if the offer already existed. They discussed apartments, her parents' likely reaction, and how much furniture two young people actually needed. Bernice insisted on a proper dining table. Matt joked they could live off milk crates.

Two days later, Ira called. "They're making you an offer. Sixty-two base. Bonus eligible. Relocation help."

Matt didn't hesitate. "I'm in."

He told his parents first. His father was stunned. His mother cried. Then he called Bernice. She screamed.

The morning after he received the official offer letter, he set off for the office. He arrived with a smile on his face as he carried a manila envelope through the marble lobby at 277 Park. His resignation letter felt heavier than paper should. The elevator ride stretched. In Stephen's office, Matt handed over the envelope.

"Are you serious?" Stephen asked, half offended.

"Absolutely. I'm leaving," Matt said.

What followed were forms, sidelong glances, and whispers. A closed-door meeting with two senior managers who tried to talk him down. A counteroffer: more money, a title bump, vague promises. It all rang hollow. Whatever had lived here for him had gone with Martin. He left the counteroffer on the desk and walked out, shoulders lighter than they'd been in months.

Two weeks later, with a suitcase and a duffel, he stood at JFK staring at the departure board. The smell of jet fuel hung in the air. Announcements crackled. He drifted through security on autopilot.

In the window seat, he watched Manhattan blur into a jagged silhouette amid the morning haze. He exhaled, not in relief, not in sorrow, but something in between. He thought of Martin. Of the bonus that never landed. Of the code they'd built. Mostly, he thought of Bernice waiting at the other end.

The plane began to taxi. Engines rose to a shout. Family, routines, the old life—all of it slid backward as the wheels left the ground.

He didn't look back. He felt both sad and excited all at once.

CHAPTER 4
LANDING

Matt's plane touched down at Hartsfield-Jackson Atlanta International Airport just as a spring storm rolled in. The clouds cracked open with a vengeance, thunder grumbling overhead, rain hammering the tarmac in sheets. As the wheels screeched against the runway and the aircraft taxied through rivers of water, Matt stared out the oval window, heart pounding with anticipation. Everything about this moment felt like a new beginning.

By the time he reached baggage claim, the storm had eased into a steady drizzle. At the top of the escalator, he saw her: Bernice, in a pale blue raincoat, hair pulled back, eyes bright even under the glaring lights. She ran toward him, her smile breaking the stale airport air. She wrapped him in a hug that dissolved weeks of doubt. For a moment, it was only her warmth, her perfume, and the soft weight of her cheek against his shoulder.

SBF had offered to cover relocation, but Matt needed little. All he asked for was a one-way flight. He and Bernice had already decided he'd move straight into her apartment.

They stepped onto the parking deck where the storm drummed on the concrete. Bernice's RAV4 coughed awake; the defroster fogged then cleared. She tuned the radio to a station that played Garth Brooks and Green Day back-to-back; Atlanta, in a single playlist. As they merged onto I-85, water fanned off truck tires, and the skyline flickered behind a gauze of rain.

"Welcome to Georgia," she said, tapping his knee twice, a habit he didn't know he'd missed until now.

That weekend, they toured used car lots under a low pewter sky, ducking between rows of aging sedans and sun-faded SUVs. One lot had a cardboard sign—$0 DOWN (OAC)—that sagged in the humidity. In Atlanta, and certainly Cobb County, cars meant survival. They test-drove a Civic that whined in second gear and a Saturn with a sunroof that wouldn't close.

Matt chose a Hyundai Excel, 60,000 miles on the odometer. The driver's window stuck unless you nudged it with your elbow, and the AC took two full minutes to kick cold—humble but reliable. He haggled for the first time in his life, palms sweating while the salesman slid a paper back and forth like a dealer in a slow game of cards.

The credit check took long enough for Bernice to braid and unbraid a strand of hair three times.

"Seven miles to Kennesaw isn't far," she said, signing her name as the co-contact for the insurance. "But without a car, it's a different planet."

They drove home with the windows cracked to clear the sweet smell of antifreeze. Rain freckled the windshield. The wipers squeaked like sneakers on a gym floor.

Bernice's apartment sat just off Marietta Square: two bedrooms, creaky hardwood, a narrow galley kitchen with a window over the sink. The air smelled faintly of pine. A rotary phone hung in the hallway; the corkboard beneath it held a neat grid of grocery lists and clipped recipes, and ceramic peaches lined a sideboard.

Her mismatched furniture somehow worked together, pastel

fabrics softening the corners. Matt noticed framed photos of Bernice at swim meets, a family Christmas shoot with her parents in matching sweaters, and a faded Polaroid of her as a child holding a golden retriever puppy. A stack of VHS tapes leaned against the TV: Sleepless in Seattle, Speed, A Few Good Men. He set his duffel down and stood a moment, listening to the apartment's small sounds: the tick of a wall clock, the whisper of air through the vent. Lived in. Hers. Almost immediately, home.

They built a quick rhythm without talking about it. Matt cooked breakfast; Bernice handled dinners. He learned which cabinet hid the good glasses and that the bathroom door needed a hip bump to latch. She learned that he folded T-shirts as if he were packing a suitcase and that he rinsed the sink after shaving until it shone. They fought once, briefly, about whether the toilet paper rolled over or under. They laughed before they could finish the argument.

On Sunday, Bernice announced they were having dinner with her parents. She called it a "gentle introduction" and ironed a shirt for him on a towel laid across the dining table.

When they arrived at her parents' home, Bernice's mother opened the door in a linen blouse and pearls, smiling with careful politeness. Her father, tall and broad-shouldered, offered a firm handshake and led Matt to the porch to point out his roses and the sprinkler schedule he swore by. Inside, iced tea sweated in a glass pitcher. Fried chicken, green beans, and cornbread came out on floral china.

The conversation was polite but probing: Where were his parents from? What did an application developer actually do? How long did he plan to stay in Georgia? Matt felt their appraisal in every glance, but Bernice's hand found his under the table, grounding him.

"You've got good manners, Mr. Hall," her mother said with a deep southern accent.

"My mom drilled them into me," Matt replied. "Couldn't leave the table until I said *thank you*."

It earned him the first genuine smile from her.

During the drive home, Bernice squeezed his knee. "They like you. They just won't admit it yet."

"You think so?"

"They do. I can tell. You make me happy, and that's all that matters to them."

On Monday morning, Matt arrived at SBF. The parking lot was a mix of pickups and sedans, with one gleaming orange Jaguar F-Type sports car. Inside, overhead lights hummed; the carpet ran in tired gray lanes. A receptionist with a headset said, "Good morning," without looking up.

Rajive Singh, head of application development, met him at reception. His shirt was pressed and sleeves rolled, giving him the appearance of relaxed efficiency. "Welcome to the madness," he said, shaking Matt's hand before leading him down the hallway past framed photos of ribbon cuttings and charity golf tournaments.

For the next hour, Rajive explained the business. SBF was a six-year-old, privately held FinTech that made its money on merchant cash advances. Technically not a loan, but close enough to make regulators squirm. After SBF's internal credit checks, a business received cash up front. SBF, in return, siphoned off roughly 10 percent of its daily credit card transactions until the advance and fees were repaid. Risky for the borrower. Lucrative for SBF. Lightly regulated for both.

Because the product lived in a legal gray zone, every system had to be built in-house, or purchased but highly customized. That's why Matt was there. Goose, their aging COBOL-based core operating platform, was straining under years of patches and shortcuts.

Rajive walked him through a door marked OPERATIONS —rows of cubicles and headsets peppered with the soft chorus of scripted greetings. "The batch happens at night," he said over the hum. "So do collections, reconciliations, and statements. Days are for originations and fires." He pointed through a glass wall to a smaller room where two analysts were wrestling with a dot-matrix printer. "And that's reporting. They think they own us."

His new teammates looked nothing like the sharp-elbowed developers at Camden. Derek, team lead, was late fifties, wearing a grubby white shirt with a coffee ring on the sleeve, and was calm to the point of sleepy. He had a habit of capping and uncapping a felt-tip pen while he thought. Ray Oh, mid-forties, South Asian, polite but distracted, wore a corded telephone headset even when he wasn't on a call, as if he might be at any second. Royland, around 40, tall and soft-spoken, greeted Matt with a two-handed shake that felt like a welcome rather than a test. They were the keepers of Goose, a system that had been built years ago and was the heart of the business. Rajive, half engineer, half diplomat, was their conductor.

"We don't build perfect code here," Rajive told him. "We build *useful* code. The trick is knowing which one matters more."

HR consumed the rest of that day in a windowless, dusty room: policies, benefits, compliance modules. They drilled one line into him until he felt the words were freighted: *a merchant cash advance is not a loan. Never call it a loan.* He signed acknowledgments that said the same thing in three different ways.

He received a login badge and a stack of loose documentation that contradicted itself within the first two pages. Someone slid a printed directory of Goose modules across his desk, along with a yellow sticky note that read, "Start here?"

By the end of his first week, Matt understood Goose was less a system than an ecosystem. Outdated docs, oral histories, and code stitched together like patchwork. He learned the AS/400's green screen shortcuts the way you learn a new city.

He quickly got to grips with the strange naming convention for each sub-component: WRKACTJOB for active transactions, DSPLOG for historical accounts, and WRKJOBSCDE for the routines that kept the whole thing running. Then there were the Night jobs, named with humor and fatalism—DUCKFEED, GANDER, HATCH. A comment in one module read simply: "DON'T TOUCH THIS. -D."

He watched as developers pushed changes straight into production, sometimes as late as midday. Twice that week, the system crashed. No one panicked. Someone would shout, "Derek, Goose is down again!" and half an hour later, the system was back, a little crooked maybe, but standing.

On Thursday, he found himself beside Derek at a terminal, while operations hovered behind them like bad weather. A batch program had deadlocked on a temporary table that wasn't temporary enough.

"See," Derek said, tapping a line with the felt-tip, "this bit is greedy. It wants everything in one bite."

"Break it up?" Matt asked.

Derek nodded once. "Chew your food."

They split the job into smaller components, eliminated a lock task, and then reran it. The queue cleared. Operations drifted away, leaving only the relief of people who had just avoided trouble.

"Nice hands," Derek said, as if Matt were a shortstop. It was the highest compliment he would get all week.

By the second week, Matt realized it wasn't disorder, exactly. The culture was strangely laid-back, and they were in control of the chaos—no barked orders, midnight fire drills, or angry emails at 2 a.m. They fixed problems instead of punishing anyone. People shrugged off mistakes. People laughed, fixed, and carried on.

He and Royland started a lunchtime ritual: a walk to the barbecue place next door for pulled pork sandwiches and a debate about whether the Braves would repeat. Ray showed Matt the good coffee machine hidden in accounting, the one that didn't spit out coffee that tasted like scorched paper. On Friday, someone brought in a sheet cake that said *WELCOME MATT* in blue frosting that dyed everyone's tongues.

Then came the email.

Dennis Robinson, CEO of SBF, asked to meet him. Panic spiked. Had he already broken some unspoken rule?

But Dennis welcomed him with a warm handshake and a glass of sweet tea in his corner office. A Georgia Bulldogs helmet sat on one shelf, and a framed Mark Twain quote on another. Through the window, heat made the parking lot wobble like a mirage.

"People matter," Dennis said, leaning back. "If I don't know who's working here, how can I expect them to care about the company?"

He asked Matt to tell him something he'd built that went wrong and what he'd learned. Matt told the truth about having had a bad deploy at Camden and a night spent undoing his own certainty.

Dennis laughed softly. "That's the scar tissue we like. You will not be bored here."

At Camden, the CEO was a name on a memo. Here, he was flesh and blood. Matt left the meeting lighter than he'd gone in.

A month in, Matt found a groove, professionally and personally. The Goose team worked like family, not rivals. The team didn't tally mistakes; they only fixed them. He wasn't grinding twelve-hour days or jolting awake at phantom pager buzzes. He and Bernice slid into a simple rhythm: Friday dinners on Marietta Square at Hemingway's, Saturday concerts at the civic center, or movies at the theater with the sticky floors. They took Sunday hikes up Kennesaw Mountain and spent evenings curled together on the sofa, VHS tapes hissing in the VCR, vinyl humming from Bernice's turntable.

Once during a storm, the power blinked, and the VCR ate *Sleepless in Seattle*. Bernice fished the tape out with a butter knife and two band aids, then declared they were switching to books for the night. Matt read to her from the *Atlanta Journal-Constitution*, stumbling on the high school sports names. She laughed and corrected his drawl.

Work had its own minor victories. Matt shaved five minutes off a reconciliation job by making a minor code change in the active memory; operations applauded as if he'd brought donuts. He wrote a plain English comment block at the top of a gnarly module that started with: "Future human: this is how it works," and Derek, passing by, capped his pen and said, "About time someone left a map."

Matt would call his parents on Sundays. His father asked about the car; his mother wanted to know if Bernice was feeding him enough. He promised to come up for Thanksgiving, and he meant it.

It was a different world from New York. Softer. Kinder. And far less aggressive.

Yet even in the quiet, he couldn't shake the sense that something waited, just out of sight, just beyond the next corner. He told himself it was ambition, the thrill that came before the next project. He told himself lots of things.

On a Monday morning in late spring, as he passed operations with a coffee, someone called out, "Goose is hiccupping again!" The word choice made him smile. Hiccups you could fix.

CHAPTER 5
ANATOMY OF A MACHINE

Life in Georgia suited Matt. The long commutes, the caffeine-fueled coding marathons, the brittle tension of the New York office; none of that followed him south. In Marietta, mornings were unhurried, the streets calm. Most days began with a slow walk to the car, birdsong in the background, and Bernice's kiss still warm on his lips. He no longer measured his value in deadlines or support tickets. His inbox didn't own him. His evenings were his again.

And SBF? It ran like a team, quite unlike his experience at Camden Bank.

By his sixth week, the Goose system was familiar ground. He'd memorized the key modules, mapped out the daily batch flow, even written a few patches to clean up error-handling logic that had been duct-taped together by predecessors. His teammates, Derek, Royland, and Ray Oh, seemed genuinely impressed.

But Matt didn't stop there.

He started asking questions. Not because anything seemed broken, but because the system felt too simple. Too crude for the volume of money it moved. Where were the fail-safes? The redundancies? The tripwires?

Everyone knew the company sold merchant cash advances. But how did it really work? Where did the money come from, and where did it go? What were the triggers, the bottlenecks, the checks and balances? After working for a bank, the lack of guardrails and systemic controls seemed just plain wrong to Matt.

So, he asked around. He read internal documentation, combed through onboarding PDFs, and flagged process flow-charts buried deep in SharePoint. The product, it turned out, was as singular as it was profitable.

SBF really did work exclusively with merchant cash advances. The one product they had mastered, the one product they offered. Instead of issuing loans, it advanced money to small businesses for a percentage of their future credit card sales. It was fast, unsecured, and highly lucrative, with minimal regulation. It also bordered on being illegal.

The key, Matt realized, was split processing. After approving a business, SBF inserted itself into the merchant's credit card pipeline. Every swipe, tap, or dip at a point-of-sale terminal sent 10 percent straight to SBF. The rest flowed to the business's own account.

Money came in every day, like clockwork.

And it didn't stop.

Curious to dig deeper, Matt asked his team who could give him a proper overview of the entire business.

"Talk to Phil Morris," Derek said without hesitation. "He's the guy. Been here since the beginning."

"Phil's weird," Ray added with a grin. "But brilliant. Walking archive."

So, Matt sent an email.

Phil replied almost instantly: *Come by anytime. I live for this stuff.*

Phil Morris was unlike anyone Matt had met at SBF. He was tall, six foot four at least, thin to the point of appearing fragile, with the perpetual look of someone who had just emerged from a library basement. His office was a jungle of stacked binders, curling printouts, half-erased whiteboards, and one lopsided bookshelf that leaned toward the window as if trying to escape.

He greeted Matt with a long handshake and a wide, toothy smile.

"I hear you've been poking around," Phil said, gesturing to a chair that creaked as Matt sat. "I like that. Curiosity's underrated."

"I just want to understand the big picture," Matt said. "I've got a handle on Goose, but I want to see how it all connects."

Phil nodded, delighted. "All right then. Welcome to the engine room."

For the next hour, Phil talked, and Matt listened. SBF had over $500 million in active transactions under management. The model revolved around velocity: approve quickly, fund quickly, and collect relentlessly.

"Our profit margins are insane," Phil said with a chuckle. "Verging on exploitative, depending on your ethics professor."

Matt raised an eyebrow. "So why do people use us?"

Phil leaned back, clearly expecting the question. He laced his fingers behind his head and smiled.

"Imagine you run a pizza shop," he said. "One morning, your ovens die. Not repairable—dead. Replacing them costs 50 grand minimum."

Matt nodded.

"You don't have that kind of cash lying around. The bank tells you to fill out an application, then makes you wait 20 days, but by then, you will be out of business. In reality, you have less than a week to get back up and running. So, you call us. We underwrite you in a day, and by the next, the money is in your account. You buy your ovens, keep your staff, keep your customers. You stay open."

Matt sat back. "Okay, but the cost?"

Phil shrugged theatrically. "We don't charge interest. It's not a loan."

Matt tilted his head. "I've heard that a dozen times now. Then what is it?"

"An unsecured advance," Phil said. "We buy a portion of your future receivables. Simple as that."

Matt narrowed his eyes. "What's the repayment in your pizza shop example?"

"Fifty advanced," Phil said. "Repay a hundred. Daily payments off the top of your credit card volume."

Matt blinked. "Double?"

Phil smiled. "We call it a 1.0 factor rate. Clients sign a purchase agreement, not a loan document. Legally, it's clean."

Matt stared at him, jaw slack.

"Look," Phil said, sensing the tension, "we're fast, we're honest, and we say yes when banks say no. Our customers know the cost. But they also know they'd be dead without the cash. It's survival capital."

Matt didn't argue. The ethics were murky, but the math was clear.

Over the next few weeks, Matt kept digging.

He requested one-on-one meetings with every department head: underwriting, legal, operations, accounting, sales, and collections. At Camden, those kinds of meetings had been political minefields. Here, doors opened easily.

He expected stress, rivalries, power plays. Instead, he found a row of seasoned pros who had been with the company for years, some since its inception. Everyone seemed relaxed, confident, and oddly content.

No one looked overworked. People laughed in meetings. Hallways were quiet. Lunches were long. Morale was high.

And everyone loved Dennis Robinson.

"He remembered my kid's birthday," one manager said.

"He sat with my mom in the hospital waiting room," said another.

Matt couldn't believe it.

"He gave me a second chance when I bombed an interview," someone added. "Hired me anyway. Told me I reminded him of himself."

It didn't take long for Matt to understand the real secret behind SBF's cultural magic: Dennis.

SBF catered lunch every Wednesday—tacos, barbecue, pasta, you name it. On Fridays, at exactly 3:00 p.m., the beer and wine came out. Everyone stopped what they were doing and toasted to the weekend. It wasn't excessive, just tradition. No one abused it.

Performance reviews were informal. Raises generous. Bonuses frequent. There were no slammed doors, no corner-office tantrums. The place ran on trust.

And money.

SBF wasn't a startup. It was a money-printing machine, humming away quietly under the guise of financial services.

By the end of his second month, Matt had built a complete mental map of how the company operated. He knew how the money flowed in, how they collected it, and how Goose reconciled it all. He also realized how little regulatory oversight existed—and that audits came only once a year.

This was a completely different beast than Camden.

CHAPTER 6
SUMMER BUZZ

By mid-June, Matt had fully settled into life in Georgia. The rhythm was easy, almost hypnotic: breakfast with Bernice at the small kitchen table, sunlight streaming through lace curtains, the smell of her cinnamon coffee filling the room. A quick drive into the office, windows cracked to let in the thick summer air. Most mornings, he was the first to arrive at Team Goose, the building still cool from overnight air conditioning. He would boot up his workstation in the quiet hum of early morning, sipping from a Styrofoam cup while the fans whispered and the fluorescent lights buzzed.

Most days, the coding didn't last long.

Some glitches in Goose's production layer would flare up, dragging them into firefighting mode. Matt would ping Derek or Royland, and within minutes they'd be shoulder to shoulder, leaning into the glow of a single monitor, tracing stack logs while muttering short curses under their breath. Ray often hovered behind, arms crossed, headset still looped around his ear even when muted. Once they patched the broken loop or squashed a bad pointer, the three men would drift back to their desks, the office settling again into a low, contented murmur, as if nothing had happened.

Matt discovered that downtime at SBF looked different. At Camden, silence was tension; at SBF, silence was simply breathing room.

Mid-morning coffee runs stretched into conversations about baseball, politics, or the best ribs in Cobb County. Derek once produced a battered deck of cards at 11:00 a.m. and roped Ray into a three-round game of spades right there at his desk. The slap of cards hitting the particleboard carried down the hall. Nobody hid it. Nobody cared. They didn't measure productivity in keystrokes. Everyone trusted Goose would keep running; or, if it didn't, someone would fix it.

Dennis, true to form, encouraged the looseness. On a humid Thursday in late June, Matt opened his inbox to find a company-wide email:

From: Dennis Robinson

Subject: Summer Dress Code Update

From July 1 to August 31, feel free to wear summer attire. T-shirts, shorts, polos, sundresses—all welcome unless you're meeting with a client. Let's stay cool and productive.

Matt grinned, picturing Camden's bankers choking on their starched collars. The idea of developers in cargo shorts and sandals on Park Avenue was unthinkable. Here, it was just common sense.

By mid-July, anticipation buzzed through the halls with news of the semiannual company meeting. The invitation promised a company update, leadership remarks, and, intriguingly, a "special message from ownership." Matt made a point of arriving early, curious to see SBF in full assembly.

The large conference room smelled faintly of carpet cleaner and barbecue from last Wednesday's catered lunch. Ten minutes before the start, people had already filled every chair. Latecomers leaned against walls, perched on filing cabinets, or sat cross-legged in corners. The lights dimmed. Conversations tapered to a hush as Dennis took the stage.

His slides were simple—white text, blue background—but the graphs spoke volumes: revenue up 20 percent year over year, operating expenses rising slower, net profit up 5 percent. Dennis' voice carried an easy Southern cadence, reassuring and measured.

"We've decided to expand the annual bonus pool," he said finally, his grin wide. "Everyone who performs will share in this success. You've earned it."

A ripple moved through the room. Smiles. Raised eyebrows. A few claps. Even the veterans straightened in their seats.

But Dennis had not finished.

He clicked through to the next slide. "I'd like to introduce someone many of you haven't met. Yet without him, none of us would be here. Please welcome Ed Cushin."

A murmur rolled through the crowd.

Ed stepped forward slowly. He was shorter than Matt expected, maybe five feet six, but immaculately put together: tailored gray suit, green silk tie with a matching pocket square, Italian loafers that glistened under the lights. His skin had the bronze sheen of a man who spent more time on boats than in offices. His age—somewhere near 60—showed only in the silver at his temples.

His voice, however, was steady, unpretentious.

"Thank you all," Ed began. "You've helped build something remarkable. Dennis and the leadership team have exceeded every target we set. But what excites me most is what comes next."

He paused, letting the silence gather.

"We've started early discussions about taking SBF public," he said at last. "Maybe as early as next year."

The room froze. Matt felt the breath catch in his chest.

Ed continued, smiling faintly. "Now, I can't guarantee this," he said. But if it does happen, everyone here will share in that success. Not just executives. Not just managers. *Everybody*."

He didn't mention stock options directly. He didn't need to. Everyone knew.

Throughout the rest of the day, whispers carried through cubicles and down the hallways. What would the shares be worth? Would there be a lockup? Could they cash out? Even the calmest veterans couldn't hide the spark in their eyes.

That evening, Matt and Bernice met at their favorite Mexican restaurant off Marietta Square. They could smell grilled onions and lime as the servers slid sizzling platters through the low-lit dining room. They squeezed into their usual booth by the window, condensation dripping down salt-rimmed margarita glasses.

Matt told her everything.

Bernice's eyes widened as he spoke. "They're talking about going public?" she asked, nearly spilling her drink.

He nodded. "Not confirmed. But Ed said if they do, everyone gets a piece."

She leaned across the table; her smile glowed in the candle-light. "That's huge, Matt. Do you realize how rare that is?"

Matt shrugged, but inside, he knew. Very rare. Almost unheard of.

"If you get shares," she whispered, her fingers brushing his across the table, "we could finally do Italy. Or even start looking to buy our own home."

The words lingered between them, sweeter than the flan on the menu. He watched the excitement on her face, the way she believed in him so instinctively—in *them*.

For years, he had measured his worth in lines of code and late nights. Now, in that small booth, with Bernice's hand resting lightly on his, he felt the future open wider than he'd ever dared to imagine.

This wasn't just a job anymore. It was a horizon.

And it might be bigger than anything he had dreamed.

CHAPTER 7
WINTER REALIZATION

T he Georgia winter arrived gently. The leaves had long
since turned, and the morning air carried a crisp edge,
but the biting cold of New York was nowhere to be found.

For Matt, it was an entirely new experience; his first winter
without layering up, without dodging slushy sidewalks or
watching taxis spray gray water onto frozen curbs.

Instead, he and Bernice would sip coffee on the apartment
balcony, watching their neighborhood stir beneath steely skies.
The air hinted at pine and chimney smoke, and the only sound
was the slow rustle of branches shaking the last of their leaves
free.

Their relationship began to mature. Weekdays began with
breakfast together: eggs, toast, sometimes fruit if Bernice had
gone to the market. The scent of her coffee, always stronger
than his, filled their little kitchen.

Matt's commute was short, a 10-minute drive in his beat-up
Hyundai, headlights cutting through the morning haze. He
enjoyed being the first one in, pulling into the empty lot with
its white painted lines glistening with dew. The office building
loomed squat and nondescript, but inside, it belonged to him in
those early hours. The lights flickered reluctantly awake as he

swiped his badge, the low rumble of the heating ducts filling the silence. His footsteps echoed on the linoleum floor. Goose's server lights blinked behind their cage, steady, indifferent, like a beast waiting for a command.

There was something eerie about the space before dawn. Too quiet. Too tidy. The faint metallic tang of hot dust lingered in the vents, and sometimes he thought he could hear the cleaning crew's cart squeak past the break room; though the building had no lower level, just long corridors and sealed offices. It gave the place a maze-like feel with hidden doors.

He used the solitude to tackle development tasks, but more often than not, Goose disrupted the calm. A batch would freeze, or a customer record would fail to update, and before long, Derek or Royland would shuffle in, steaming mugs in hand. Derek had a way of appearing without a sound, like a ghost in mismatched flannel and sagging jeans, his scruffy beard peppered with gray. He always seemed as if he needed a shower. He'd lean over Matt's screen with a faint smirk, unconcerned.

"Been doing that since before you got here," he'd mutter, as if Goose's glitches were just part of the weather. Nothing surprised him. Nothing rattled him.

Royland, taller and more deliberate, would roll up beside them, his deep voice cutting calmly through the lines of code. Together, they'd patch, re-route, or reset, then drift back to their desks. Within minutes, it was as if nothing had happened at all.

Some mornings, they fixed very little until after lunch, and yet, Goose kept running. That was the culture: loose, forgiving, laid-back. Unlike at Camden, where failure meant stress, here, it meant shrugging and another cup of coffee. And when things were quiet, the mood relaxed even more. Nobody hid it; nobody cared. Goose had its own rhythm, and the people had learned to sway with it.

Dennis continued to encourage the laid-back culture—in his own way. In mid-December, he sent another email across the company:

From: Dennis Robinson

Subject: Holiday Party—Let's Celebrate!

Friends, it's been an extraordinary year. Let's end it right. On December 22nd, we'll host the company's biggest holiday party yet: private event space near Marietta Square, dinner catered, open bar, live band. No speeches, no suits. Just food, laughter, and a chance to enjoy each other's company. You've earned it.

Excitement buzzed through the office for days. Matt watched grown men argue over what song the band might play first. Even Derek cracked a smile and promised to wear his "holiday best."

The day of the event arrived quickly, and inside, the party itself shimmered. Strands of white lights decorated the unique venue, a converted cotton warehouse with high ceilings and exposed beams. The smell of roasted meat and spiced cider filled the air. Bernice stunned in a forest green cocktail dress that seemed to draw every eye in the room. Matt couldn't count the compliments she fielded. Derek turned up in a sweater festooned with blinking Christmas lights, grinning awkwardly as people laughed with him, not at him. Ray Oh had bourbon in both hands before the salad course. Matt saw everyone loosen completely, laughter rising against the live band's jazzy take on carols.

Bernice pressed close to him on the dance floor, whispering in his ear, "This doesn't feel like work. It feels like family."

And for a moment, Matt let himself believe it.

But outside the warmth of parties and shared toasts, life kept moving. Their apartment, once cozy, now felt cramped. One Sunday, wandering through Marietta Square with steaming cups of hot chocolate, Bernice stopped at a sales office for a new townhouse development.

"Want to look?" she asked, her eyes glinting in the winter light.

Matt agreed. The model home smelled faintly of fresh paint, hardwood floors gleaming under recessed lights. The ceilings soared, promising air and room to grow. By Christmas Eve, they had signed papers, put down a deposit, and tucked away the builder's projection: ready by summer. Bernice whispered, almost reverently, "By next July, it'll be ours."

At the same time, Bernice's career had taken a step forward. Recently promoted to human resources, she now had more autonomy, better hours, and a new spark in her eyes each evening when she came home. Matt was proud, genuinely proud. But beneath it lingered something else: envy. She was rising, while he was idling.

Because the truth was, he was bored.

SBF was calm. Too calm. It lacked challenge. After the chaos and pressure of Camden, the late-night fire drills, the stakes that sharpened every line of code, this felt like drifting. He had thought he wanted peace, but now peace felt like stagnation.

One chilly morning just before Christmas, Matt lingered alone at his desk. The sun had barely risen, a dull blue light seeping across the parking lot. His coffee sat cooling, untouched. With no deadlines, no urgent requests, no one breathing down his neck, he opened Goose's code repository almost absently, scrolling through modules he already knew by heart.

Then he saw it.

A routing function. Clean. Elegant. Too elegant.

There were no reconciliation checks. No secondary logs. No validation comparing expected versus actual payouts. Because the system relied on percentages of card settlements, there was no fixed target, no backstop. It just accepted the flow, distributed funds, and moved on.

Matt frowned. He traced it upstream. Then downstream. It was always the same: no guardrails, no controls, and no double checks anywhere in the system.

Derek's words echoed in his head: "Been like that since before SBF even had a name."

The air suddenly felt thinner. His chest tightened.

Not that the code was wrong. It was that it was blind. And nobody seemed to mind.

A memory surfaced: Derek's desk, always tidy. Yet once, passing behind, Matt had glimpsed a strange command window open on his terminal. Nothing Goose-related. When asked, Derek had chuckled and said, "Just Spring cleaning." Matt had thought little of it then. Now, the phrase scratched at him.

Earlier that week, a transaction batch had shown a negative variance. Ray Oh had waved it off as a timestamp error, but the audit trail looked ... too clean, as if someone had designed code to smooth over a crack rather than seal it.

Curiosity took hold. Matt ran a report on payout distributions over the last 18 months. On the surface, the data appeared to be good. Too good. The variance in settlement timing was nearly identical from month to month. Not impossible. But improbable—and that set his instincts buzzing.

At Camden, this would have triggered alarms. At SBF, no one even blinked.

That night, after dinner and a long, tender evening with Bernice, he lay awake, her breath steady against his chest. His mind churned. The absence of reconciliation wasn't an oversight. It was culture, built into the company's DNA. Goose had always run that way, and Derek had helped write it.

If someone had exploited the gap ... would anyone even know?
Would he?

The thought unsettled him, not from fear, but from unease, like hearing the first crack echo underfoot while walking on ice.

He turned on his side, staring at the dark ceiling. Derek's calmness. The "spring cleaning" window. The flawless audit trail. Pieces drifted together.

He wasn't thinking about fraud. Not yet, but based upon his experiences at Camden, something did not feel right. There was just no systemic oversight.

He started thinking about how easy it would be for him to rig the system. To prove its weakness. To be the one who saw what no one else seemed to see—almost like a favor to SBF.

And that realization bothered him more than he wanted to admit. Was he really smarter than the rest of the team?

Sleep came eventually, but it brought no comfort.

Only questions.

CHAPTER 8
PROMISE AND ITCH

B ecause of the nature of its business, SBF had to remain open through Christmas. Daily credit card payments didn't stop just because it was the holidays; in fact, the volume of transactions increased, and merchants still expected their accounts to be updated. But the company scaled down to a skeleton crew during the final two weeks of the year, with each department rotating minimal staff to keep operations humming.

For the Goose team, this meant drawing straws, or in this case, quietly volunteering. Royland offered to cover the week between Christmas and New Year's, freeing up Matt and the rest of the team to enjoy a proper break. Matt was grateful. He hadn't been back to New York since moving down to Georgia, and the timing was perfect to spend some long-overdue time with his parents.

He convinced Bernice to come along.

They flew Delta into JFK a few days before Christmas. The flight was calm. The cabin dimmed after takeoff as the hum of the engines became a kind of white noise. Once the drink service made its rounds, they sat with two plastic cups of red wine balanced on the tray table. Outside the oval window, clouds glowed faintly against the moonlight, a quilt of silver and shadow.

"I've been thinking," Matt said, voice low, the tone people use when they're half afraid of the answer.

Bernice raised an eyebrow. "Uh-oh."

"No, good thinking," he said quickly, smiling nervously. "About us. About the house. And maybe getting engaged."

Bernice froze for a beat, eyes wide, and let out a scream. She hadn't seen it coming. But then, just as quickly, her expression softened. She leaned in and kissed him, her lips warm and sure, the taste of cheap cabernet on both of their tongues.

"Let's do it," she whispered, her voice trembling with a mixture of surprise and wonder. She rested her forehead against his, her fingers tightening around his hand. "I've been waiting for you to say that."

The remaining hour of the flight passed in near silence, both of them smiling in disbelief, exchanging glances as if to confirm that yes, this was real. The kind of silence that buzzed with energy.

As they collected their bags, Matt leaned in. "Let's keep it between us for now. At least until I discuss it with your dad and get his approval."

Bernice nodded, slipping her arm through his. "Good idea; he would love the old-fashioned approach."

Matt's parents lived in a modest two-story house in Bay Ridge, Brooklyn. The neighborhood was decorated for the season with glowing reindeer on stoops, crookedly hung wreaths on row house doors, and kids in puffy jackets dragging sleds over bare sidewalks, hoping for the elusive snow.

His mother welcomed them with a warm hug and a roast already in the oven. The house smelled of rosemary and garlic. His father shook Bernice's hand, then pulled her into an unexpected bear hug, laughing at Matt's raised eyebrows. Over two nights, they fell in love with her. She was charming, thoughtful, and brought out a lighter, more affectionate side of Matt that they hadn't seen in years.

Even his older sister, Clare—famously critical of every girl-friend Matt had ever brought home—approved. She and Bernice talked for hours over coffee and pastries at the kitchen table, leaning close as if they'd known each other forever. By the time they left, Clare hugged her goodbye like an old friend.

But Matt and Bernice never mentioned the engagement. That secret lived quietly between them, like a spark tucked into their pockets.

On the return flight to Atlanta, Matt brought it up again somewhere over the Appalachians.

"I'll talk to your dad over New Year's," he said.

Bernice squeezed his hand, her nails lightly pressing into his skin. "Don't wait too long. I want to wear the ring already."

New Year's Eve arrived clear and cold.

Marietta Square had transformed into a Christmas post-card: fairy lights strung across storefronts, trees wrapped in twinkling strands, vendors selling mulled wine, hot chocolate, and handmade ornaments that smelled faintly of pine sap. Carolers in wool scarves sang beside a local brass band playing Christmas carols near the gazebo, their notes sharp in the cool night air. Couples huddled together under blankets on the grass. A light breeze carried the scent of cinnamon and wood smoke.

Matt and Bernice had become regulars at Hemingway's and knew most of the bar staff by name. That night, they bar-hopped with a small group of friends they'd gradually built up, a mix of Bernice's coworkers, their neighbors, and one or two from Matt's office. There were shots, champagne toasts, and a half-hearted countdown shouted through slurred voices. At midnight, the square was full of drunken revelers, and in the distance, someone was letting off fireworks that popped like muffled cannon fire above the rooftops.

On New Year's Day, they woke late and groggy, their bodies still recovering from the previous night's indulgences. The sun had already climbed high, flooding the bedroom with a sharp winter glare that made them squint against their hangovers.

They shuffled into the kitchen where Bernice, barefoot and bleary-eyed, fumbled through the cupboard for Advil. Matt brewed a pot of overly strong coffee, the bitter steam filling the apartment like a lifeline. They sat at the small kitchen table in silence, each nursing a mug and a headache as they listened to the tick of the wall clock and the hiss of the radiator. The joy of the night before lingered faintly, but so did the dull ache of reality creeping back in.

Bernice's parents invited them to dinner that afternoon. Their house was filled with the aroma of sage and turkey, greeting them the moment they walked in. Her parents had formally set the table, the roast steaming and cranberry sauce in delicate ceramic bowls. Her mother wore pearls. Her father wore a cardigan with elbow patches, his expression warm but watchful.

After dessert, while Bernice was in the kitchen helping her mom, Matt stood and asked her father, Frank, if they could talk privately. He led him to the porch, where the air was sharp, every breath clouding in the January air.

"Sir," Matt began, his voice catching slightly as he shifted his weight from foot to foot, hands jammed nervously into his coat pockets. "I've been wanting to speak with you for a while, but, well, I'm not great with words. I love your daughter. She means everything to me. And I'd like your blessing to marry her."

Frank looked at him for a long moment, face unreadable, the silence stretching just long enough for Matt to feel the pulse in his ears.

Then he nodded. "You're a good man, Matt. Yes, with our blessing and support. You make our little girl very happy."

Matt exhaled and smiled, his nerves just beginning to settle when Frank added, "If that ever stops, I'll be coming for you, well, actually not me personally; I will pay someone."

There was a hint of a smile on the older man's face, but his tone was level, just serious enough to make Matt wonder. Was it a joke? A protective father's warning? Or both? Either way, the message landed. Matt gave a slight nod, the weight of responsibility settling on his shoulders like a new coat.

Inside, when they told her mother, she screamed so loudly that Bernice came rushing back into the room. She immediately guessed what had happened, beaming as her mother hugged them both, tears sparkling in her eyes.

The next morning, Matt called his parents with the news. His mother squealed, his father chuckled, and Clare demanded every detail.

The glow of the holiday lasted just a few more days.

———

WHEN MATT RETURNED TO WORK, the office was quiet, the halls still dotted with leftover tinsel and a few unopened boxes of candy canes. Royland gave him a quick rundown of anything urgent, but there wasn't much. Goose had behaved. The lights were on. No fires to put out.

Royland had manned the office over the break. He told Matt that "Derek came in a few times, unannounced, just drifted in and out like a ghost. Mostly sat back and babysat the system, didn't even open half his usual tools."

That struck Matt as odd. Derek rarely showed up for appearance's sake. He worked either deeply or not at all. Babysitting wasn't his style.

He sat at his desk and stared at the three-monitor setup in front of him. The logs showed no hiccups. All batch jobs had completed. The payment gateway had synced on time, and the merchant reporting feeds were clean. Everything looked perfect. Too perfect.

Matt could not stop thinking about how the whole system was flawed. Yes, SBF made lots of money, but to Matt, the operational and technical platforms felt like a house of cards. He kept returning to Goose, back to the codebase that still lacked basic checks. Back to the function, he couldn't stop thinking about. He'd traced it again after the holidays, and nothing had changed. No one seemed to care; if they even knew.

Maybe that was the problem. He cared too much. Or maybe ... he just understood it better than anyone else. Either way, the itch was there.

That night, Matt lay awake, staring at the ceiling. Bernice's breathing was soft beside him, but his mind wouldn't quiet.

The absence of reconciliation wasn't an oversight. It was systemic. Built into the company's DNA. Everyone accepted it. Goose had been around from the beginning, and Derek had helped write it.

But he was thinking about how the system was so flawed, so open to abuse, that the company was running a major risk, probably one they did not know really existed. Should he be the one to prove it? To beat it? If he brought it up with Derek or management, they'd probably just shrug. The place was too laid-back, too used to letting things slide. That was the culture. No one seemed to want to fix what they didn't even acknowledge as broken.

And that bothered him more than he wanted to admit.

CHAPTER 9
SIGNALS

The first week of January was a slow one at SBF. The holidays had taken the wind out of everyone's sails, and now, back at their desks, the Goose team found themselves surrounded by the familiar whir of monitors and the soft drip of the coffeepot, but did not have much to do.

Outside, winter sunlight slanted weakly through narrow blinds, casting pale stripes across their shared cubicles.

With the four-person team all seated together, Royland leaned back in his chair, absently tossing a foam stress ball into the air.

"So, what'd you all get up to over the break?" he asked, his voice casual but carrying easily in the quiet.

Derek, who looked as if he had just rolled out of bed, grunted and said, "Not much."

Ray told the group he was glad to be back at work after staying with his sister and her four kids for a few days. He mimed pulling out his hair to make the others laugh.

Royland looked at Matt. "Anything exciting?"

Matt hesitated. He wasn't someone who liked the spotlight. But after a beat, he smiled shyly and said, "Actually ... Bernice and I got engaged."

The reaction was instantaneous. Royland jumped up and clapped him on the shoulder hard enough to rattle his chair. Derek followed with a wide grin and a hearty handshake, surprising in its firmness, while Ray gave him a dramatic bow before launching into a half-serious monologue about the end of freedom and how marriage was a life sentence with no parole.

The jokes came fast and free:

"Kiss your video game time goodbye."

"Hope you like HGTV and murder mystery programs."

"Better practice saying, 'yes dear' now."

Beneath the banter, though, there was genuine warmth.

"Congrats, man," Royland said with a sincere nod. "She's a keeper."

"That girl's got class," Ray added. "Don't screw it up."

"Rather you than me," Derek muttered, but even that came with a crooked smile.

Matt laughed and tried to brush off the attention, but it didn't end there. Later that afternoon, Dennis popped by his desk unannounced, as usual, and gave Matt a firm pat on the back.

"Well done, man," he said, flashing a grin. "I hear you're finally going to make an honest woman out of that beautiful girlfriend of yours. Good call."

Matt blinked. He hadn't told Dennis. He hadn't even told HR. Word had somehow spread like wildfire. Everywhere he went for the rest of the day, from the break room to the developer bullpen, people congratulated him.

Just before 4 p.m., Matt's name crackled across the building-wide speaker system.

"Attention, everyone," Dennis' voice boomed with mock ceremony. "Let it be known that our very own Matt Hall is officially off the market. Congratulations to Matt and Bernice on their engagement!"

A wave of laughter and applause echoed across the floor. Matt turned beet red. From two rows over, someone shouted, "Damn, that's some next-level HR onboarding!"

"He'll never live this down," Royland said, grinning.

"Congrats, Romeo!" someone called from the other side of the bullpen.

That evening, Matt joked to Bernice, "Well, I guess I don't need to send a memo. The building already knows."

"You're practically front-page news," she teased, squeezing his hand.

They went out to celebrate at Hemingway's again, sipping wine and sharing flatbreads while friends came over one by one to toast their news.

Over the next few days, between calls to Bernice's extended family and a flurry of congratulatory texts, Matt made time to visit a jewelry shop near the square. The bell above the door jingled as he stepped inside, and he was greeted by the velvet-lined display cases glowing under the soft lights.

He didn't know what he was doing; fortunately, the woman behind the counter did.

She walked him patiently through diamonds, cuts, clarity ratings, settings, and costs, pulling trays from beneath the glass with quiet authority. In the end, he chose a mid-priced, vintage-inspired ring with an oval diamond on a slim platinum band. Understated. Elegant. Perfect.

It had taken nearly all his savings, but it was worth it.

With the ring secured and stashed in his nightstand drawer, Matt and Bernice began sketching out wedding plans. They traded ideas over dinner and late-night wine, napkins filling up with doodles of table layouts and scribbled guest lists. Spring or fall? Big ceremony or small gathering?

Matt found himself enjoying the process more than expected. It gave shape to the year ahead—something solid to move toward.

But one night, while flipping through a wedding venue brochure Bernice had picked up, the mood shifted. She pointed to a lakeside estate with wraparound porches and string lights woven through pine trees.

"This is the one," she said, eyes shining. "But it's not cheap."

Matt studied the price. It was over six months of his take-home pay.

"Maybe we aim a little lower," he said gently.

Bernice's smile faltered for just a second.

"We don't have to decide now. My parents will cover most of it." She paused, then added softly,

"I know your folks aren't in a position to do much, and that's okay, Matt. They've done enough just getting you through school."

Matt looked away, a twinge of shame running through him. He knew she meant nothing by it, but even so, it stung, and the air between them grew faintly taut.

They didn't talk about it again that night, but the tension lingered, quiet, unspoken, hovering over the wineglasses.

Back at work, Matt noticed a post-holiday surge after their first slow week. Payment logs within Goose showed merchant volumes spiking, repayments flowing thick and fast. Business was booming.

Dennis sent a company-wide email in mid-January announcing the bonus evaluation window:

Performance reviews open now. Bonus allocations announced end of February. Bigger pool this year. You've all earned it.

The buzz around the office electrified again. Conversations in the break room veered into speculation. Would the bonus really top last year's? Would Dennis surprise them again with an early payout?

The other major topic was the IPO. Ever since Ed Cushin had mentioned it at the semiannual update, the rumor mill hadn't stopped.

Matt overheard Royland at lunch: "I heard Ed met with another group of bankers from New York. That's twice this month."

"You don't keep meeting with those guys unless you're serious," Ray replied.

"When we list, and we all get a piece ..." Royland trailed off, eyes distant. Derek just raised an eyebrow and muttered, "We shall see."

The optimism was contagious. But for Matt, the excitement didn't last. His work felt increasingly mechanical. Goose needed little fixing. There were no new development initiatives. Derek kept the interesting tasks for himself. Ray and Royland seemed happy enough responding to support tickets and surfing the internet.

One morning, bored, Matt scanned a batch of logs for the fourth time that week. The itch was back.

He turned to Derek. "Hey, just curious, why isn't there any auto-reconciliation built into Goose? I mean, nothing compares expected payouts to actual receipts?"

Derek didn't look up from his terminal. "Never a requirement. Been that way since the start. The system works as designed. If it isn't broke ..."

Matt nodded but didn't reply. It wasn't wrong. But it wasn't safe either. A system could function perfectly and still be fragile. Or exploitable.

That night after dinner with Bernice, Matt booted up his laptop and reopened a set of test logs he'd pulled earlier. The apartment was dimly lit, with the TV murmuring in the background, as Bernice curled up on the sofa.

Exploring, he told himself. *Not looking for trouble.*

He observed the flow of batches, the routing of funds, and whether the totals matched. Most of it checked out. But every so often, he noticed minor variances. A dollar here. A few cents there. It was always just within the margin of error—but consistent. Nothing was provably wrong. But still, something was off; he just couldn't place it.

Matt leaned back and rubbed his temples. He sat in the glow of his monitor, the cursor blinking like a pulse.

Bernice padded in, hair loose, holding a blanket around her shoulders. "You're still working?"

"Just poking around."

"If it's not urgent, shut it down. Come over here. I'm not having my man distracted."

For the next few hours, they curled up on the sofa watching TV. A commercial came on for Caribbean cruises—turquoise water, white sand, smiling couples sipping drinks under palm trees.

Bernice nudged him. "That's it. Honeymoon goal. Antigua or St. Lucia."

Matt chuckled, but his eyes lingered on the screen. "That looks like it's going to be well out of our price range," he said.

"We can always take out a loan; it's our honeymoon, a once-in-a-lifetime trip," she countered.

Later that night, after Bernice had fallen asleep, Matt reopened his laptop. One batch file from December caught his eye. The totals didn't align. Not dramatically, but just enough to be interesting. He traced the transaction backward. The overage didn't go to SBF's account. It simply vanished. Or, more precisely, someone had rounded it away.

Not broken. Just vulnerable.

He made a note in a local file: verify decimal overflow handling in payment module. Then, almost on impulse, he cloned a copy of the distribution module and saved it under a different name, just in case.

Sleep came late that night. And not easily.

CHAPTER 10
TEST

B y the end of January, the office had fully returned to its usual rhythm. Goose was stable, business was brisk, and everyone was smoothly coasting along. Too smoothly, Matt thought.

For all the success the company touted, the actual work being done on the technical side felt oddly ... hollow. Projects moved slowly. Tickets were minor. And the few meetings they had were recycled talking points from the fall.

The Goose team cubicles felt like a forgotten outpost at the rear of the building. Overhead, the old fluorescent tubes faintly buzzed and vibrated. The whir of desktop fans blended with the quiet clatter of keyboards and the indistinct murmur of voices on speakerphones drifting from nearby departments. The air swirled with the tang of Derek's perpetual supply of beef jerky and Royland's overly spiced lentil stew, which he had just reheated.

Classic rock drifted from a small Bluetooth speaker near Ray's monitor, just loud enough to provide background but low enough to avoid complaints. A dusty ceiling vent blew recycled air that was both cold and dry, raising goosebumps on Matt's forearms. Boxes of unused cables, cracked software manuals, and spare keyboards lined the shelving along the back wall like forgotten relics of a bygone era.

There was no real stress. No pressure. Just a dull thrum of quiet repetition, which quickly turned to boredom. And for Matt, that was the problem.

Boredom was dangerous.

He could not resist scratching that itch. It wasn't malicious. Not even planned, really. Just ... curiosity.

The idea came to him late one afternoon as he stared at Goose's transaction logs. Credit card repayments trickled in around the clock: dozens of small payments per hour, each tied to a merchant account, all feeding into the main pool and then redistributed across SBF's internal ledgers. He zoomed in on the numbers, his eyes following their relentless rhythm. Again, he noticed how loose it all was. No auto-reconciliation. No redundancy checks. Just trust in the flow being accurate.

So, he wrote a script. His motivation was not driven by some desire to commit fraud, more an attempt to keep his mind active, to prove to himself, and potentially the executives at SBF, how smart he was.

It was simple. Elegant, even. He would siphon off 10 cents from every tenth transaction processed through the system, an amount insufficient to trigger alarms or exceed margin thresholds, and then quietly redirect these small amounts to a dummy account he created deep within Goose's architecture. The account didn't appear on any standard reporting dashboards and didn't trigger alerts. It was, for all intents and purposes, invisible.

He called the function *ghost10.test*.

Matt stared at the code for a while after writing it, the cursor blinking like a heartbeat on the terminal. His palms were damp, and the sound of his own breathing seemed loud in the quiet office. Finally, he ran the test in the development environment. It worked. Flawlessly. Ten cents skimmed. Every 10th transaction. Always remaining unnoticed.

The next morning, he came in early. Earlier than usual, and full of anticipation. He wanted to push the code live.

The office was quiet at 7:30 a.m. Only the janitor was there, mopping the tile floors, the sharp scent of disinfectant trailing behind him. Matt swiped in, the badge reader's beep echoing in the stillness, and made his way to his desk. This morning, he had treated himself to a Dunkin' Donuts almond-flavored coffee, which he held in one hand. His heart pounded in his chest, every step toward his workstation feeling heavier than usual.

After glancing over his shoulder to confirm the room was empty, he opened his terminal and navigated to the live deployment environment. His fingers hovered over the keyboard. His pulse thudded in his ears.

Then he heard a voice.

"Matt. Got a second?"

He jumped—literally flinched in his chair, nearly spilling the coffee across his desk.

It was Richard Eastman, the CTO. A rare sight in the Goose area. Tall, late fifties, with salt-and-pepper hair and a permanent smirk. He wore a charcoal sport coat over jeans and carried a leather notebook tucked under his arm.

"Sure," Matt said, his throat dry and heart hammering.

Richard pulled up a chair and sat down, glancing at Matt's screen before Matt had the chance to minimize the terminal. Just lines of code. Nothing incriminating. Nothing obvious. But Matt felt exposed, as if the monitor's glow were a spotlight.

"Just wanted to check in," Richard said casually. "We're looking ahead at Q2 deliverables. Dennis mentioned you might be someone to lean on for new tooling. You've got a good rep. Quiet guy, but sharp."

Matt nodded, trying to swallow the lump in his throat. "Thanks. Yeah, just ... trying to stay productive."

"That's what I like to hear." Richard smiled. "We'll be spinning up some enhancements to the risk interface soon. Maybe loop you in."

"Sounds great," Matt croaked.

Richard stood. "All right, I didn't mean to derail your morning. Catch you later."

And just like that, he was gone.

Matt sat frozen, staring at the code. The room seemed to close in on him. After five minutes of internal debate, he convinced himself to push the code into production. At 8:11 a.m., the *ghostio.test* script went live.

The day dragged. Every sound, including the ding of incoming messages on the internal messaging app, Derek's keyboard clacking in bursts, and the occasional laugh from the bullpen, was magnified. Each pop-up notification, every casual voice behind him, sent a jolt of panic through his chest.

But no one said anything. There were no alerts, no alarms, no support tickets. The silence was both a relief and a torment.

That afternoon, Derek called a quick team meeting.

He gathered everyone around his desk and handed out printouts of the new merchant onboarding procedures.

Matt sat with the others, pulse still elevated.

"Okay," Derek said, tapping his pen. "Couple of small updates."

He paused for a beat too long.

"Did someone push something to prod this morning?" His eyes flicked briefly toward Matt. "Logs were spitting out a few anomalies."

Matt felt his stomach flip.

The others barely noticed. But to Matt, it sounded loaded, as if Derek knew. As if they all did. But no one answered, and Matt's face grew hot.

Derek's expression didn't change. He simply added, "Just to make it very explicit, no one is to make any production system changes unless they clear them with me."

Ray and Royland both said, "Okay."

Matt forced himself to nod. "Understood."

Back at his desk, the feeling lingered. He rechecked the Goose logs. Nothing odd. No alerts. But his heart kept racing.

That night, he barely touched his dinner.

"You okay?" Bernice asked.

She had made lemon chicken with rosemary potatoes and a salad, their usual midweek comfort meal, but Matt only pushed the food around his plate.

"Yeah," he blurted. "Just tired."

"You've been weird all day."

"It's nothing. Just ... work stuff."

Bernice studied him for a moment; concern was etched on her brow. She turned back to her plate, unconvinced.

Later, they moved to the couch, wine in hand, with soft music playing in the background. Typically, this was their time, when stress melted away, when laughter and intimacy filled the evening.

But when Bernice leaned in and ran her fingers down Matt's chest, he gently pulled back.

"Not tonight," he said.

She blinked. "Are you sick?"

"No, just ... in my head a little."

"You're not going off me, are you?" she asked softly.

"Don't be silly," he said quickly. "It's just work."

She frowned but didn't push.

Instead, she curled against him, resting her head on his shoulder.

"Whatever it is," she whispered, "I hope it passes."

Matt didn't respond. He stared straight ahead, a bead of sweat rolling down his temple.

That night, after Bernice had fallen asleep, he crept barefoot into the living room. The apartment was silent except for the hum of the refrigerator.

He opened his laptop, logged into Goose, and checked the logs again. Line after line of transactions, all clean. Nothing flagged. Even so, he checked them again. And again. Just in case.

He sat in the screen's glow, scrolling with a sick feeling in his stomach, as if he were watching a fuse burn slowly toward an unseen charge.

He had told himself it wasn't illegal. Technically, it wasn't even against policy—there were no controls at SBF, no peer reviews, no release committee.

But it wasn't *nothing*, either.

He thought he'd feel clever. He thought he'd feel satisfaction after being overlooked, after being forced to scrape by when the firm profited from his skill—from his code. Instead, he felt sick.

He planned to let the script run for five days. He would check the dummy account on Friday evening. If it had a balance, that meant it worked. If someone had flagged it before then ... well, he'd cross that bridge when he got there.

THREE NIGHTS EARLIER, before the script, before the panic, Matt had taken Bernice to dinner at The Longleaf, a cozy southern-fusion restaurant near the square.

They had a corner booth, flickering candles, and a shared dessert of bourbon pecan pie.

After coffee, Matt reached into his jacket pocket and pulled out the small box.

"So," he said, sliding it across the table, "I think this is overdue."

Bernice opened it, gasped, and brought a hand to her mouth.

"Matt ..."

"I know you already said yes. But I wanted to do it properly."

She stared at the ring—white gold with a sapphire halo—then looked up and smiled.

"Ask me again."

He grinned. "Bernice Marie Caldwell, will you marry me?"

"Yes," she whispered.

She leaned across the table and kissed him. The waitress, returning with their check, stopped and beamed.

"Congratulations," she said, setting the bill down. "That's a beautiful ring."

Matt smiled and held Bernice's hand as she slipped it on.

For a while that evening, everything had felt right.

Later, as they walked hand in hand back to the car, Bernice squeezed his arm. "My parents are thrilled," she said. "Mom's already hinting about doing it up big, maybe even at the Country Club."

Matt nodded, forcing a smile. He hadn't said it aloud, but there was a quiet understanding between them: her family would cover the majority of the wedding costs. His parents, proud as they were, had already stretched to support his education. A wedding was beyond their means. He hadn't even asked.

"You think your mom and dad will be okay with everything?" Bernice asked.

"They'll be happy for us," he said after a pause. "I'm just not sure how much they can help with the actual wedding stuff."

Bernice kissed his cheek. "It's okay. We'll figure it out. It doesn't have to be huge."

Still, the thought nagged at him. He hated feeling as if he couldn't contribute more. And it only added to the low thrum of pressure building inside him—from work, to secrets, and now the expectations he wasn't sure he could meet.

That night, Matt didn't sleep. Each time he closed his eyes, he saw Goose's logs scrolling past, 10-cent fragments leaking like water through a hairline crack. Silent. Invisible.

And now it was real.

The test had begun.

CHAPTER 11
PENNIES

Matt arrived early the next morning, the sky still tinted with the pinkish hue of dawn. The SBF building stood quiet, its glass frontage reflecting a sleepy strip mall and two dog walkers in puffy coats. Inside, the lights flickered awake, and the HVAC whispered along the ceiling. Someone had beaten him in. Probably Derek.

He slipped into his cubicle, heart already pounding, and woke his PC. The login screen blinked back at him like a dare. When the desktop loaded, he opened a terminal and typed the sequence he'd rehearsed three times in the car.

$210.60.

His breath caught. His palms prickled; his stomach lurched. The urge to head straight to the bathroom was immediate and ridiculous, and he almost laughed. It had worked. Real transactions had skimmed and landed exactly where they were supposed to: the dummy account he'd buried inside Goose.

Yesterday, he'd finished the last lines of code with clammy hands, walking each branch and edge case twice, then once more out of superstition. Pushing to production had felt like lighting a fuse and walking away. Now, 20 hours in, nothing had blown. The log was clean. Monitoring was quiet—just a smooth test. At least, that's what Matt kept telling himself.

He stared at the number until it stopped vibrating. Pressure bloomed behind his eyes, and a low throb threatened a headache. He hovered his mouse over the kill script he'd written. One click, and the whole thing would vanish. *Back out or go forward*, he told himself. His conscience nagged at him like a draft under a door.

He got up, walked to the pantry, and downed two paper cups of coffee, each more bitter than the last. His stomach clenched, not from caffeine, he knew, but from the decision. He made a second trip to the bathroom, splashed cold water on his face, returned to his desk, closed the kill script, and let the code run.

By 8:30, the bullpen filled in its usual tide. Derek muttered at the authentication server and tapped his keyboard in short bursts. Ray lobbed a dry joke about the front-end team "breaking more than they fixed" and then, as always, chuckled at his own line. Royland tapped out a card game on his monitor and sang a snatch of a chorus under his breath that never seemed to land on the next verse—business as usual.

Matt was nowhere near his usual self. His leg bounced like a metronome under the desk. Every few minutes, he took an unnecessary lap—operations, QA, legal, marketing—just enough to seem purposeful, not enough to invite questions. Phones rang in brief flares. Printers coughed out reports. Someone reheated sausage biscuits. A fog of grease settled over the hallway.

He watched Phil Morris the closest. If anyone would catch a discrepancy, it was Phil; the man moved through numbers like a surgeon through a chest cavity. When Matt drifted past Phil's door, Phil sat hunched over his desk, fingers moving in a quick, even rhythm. No panic in his posture. No raised voice. Just the soft clack of keys and the squeak of his rolling chair.

Matt hovered, feigning nonchalance. "Everything smooth in your world today?"

Phil didn't look up. "Define smooth."

"No fires? No freak errors?"

Phil exhaled through his nose. "Not yet. But give the front-end team some time. They've never disappointed me."

Matt laughed louder than he meant to and kept moving. A sharp pang jabbed under his ribs—guilt or fear, he couldn't tell.

On his third pass through the Goose bullpen, Royland glanced up with a half-smile. "What's up, sir? Got ants in your pants?"

"Just restless. Too much coffee," Matt said.

"More like too much of something else," Royland grinned. "Tell her to let you get some sleep."

Derek smirked without looking away from his screen. "It'll all stop once you're married, anyway."

Matt hesitated. How would Derek know that? The man lived with his eighty-five-year-old mother and had never been married. But it was Derek's eyes that stuck, how they lingered a half heartbeat too long, as if he were reading a reflection on a dark window.

At 10:15, Derek raised his pen without turning. "Quick stand-up," he said, which in Goose-speak meant "turn around in your chair." No one stood.

"Couple of small updates," Derek went on, tapping a print-out. "The Front-end team is pushing a template change for onboarding—shouldn't touch us, but if you see malformed merchant IDs in the feed, holler. Also," he paused long enough for the room to notice, "logs burped a few anomalies right after eight yesterday. Nothing sustained, just ... keep an eye out."

Ray nodded. "So, just like we do every day ending in 'y'?"

Derek's mouth twitched. "If you push anything to prod, clear it with me first," he said again. His eyes flicked briefly to Matt's monitor and away again. "That's it."

By noon, Matt believed he'd gotten away with it. Dennis strolled down the aisle with his usual dad jokes and double-finger guns. The Goose crew broke for cards, ankles crossed under chairs, aces slapped with performative disgust. Phil stayed welded to his chair, married to the spreadsheet of the week.

Normal. Everything was normal. Matt's pulse said otherwise.

He forced himself to eat at his desk, microwave leftovers, a plastic fork, and a taste of cardboard he barely noticed. He opened the transaction view on a side monitor and let the lines scroll as if they were scenery out a train window. Every 10th entry, a tiny, nearly theoretical slice was whisked away to nowhere anyone could see. The logic was as simple as a magic trick: it worked because no one expected it.

At 1:40, Matt found Phil in the break room, coaxing a fresh pot of coffee from the machine, not trusting it to do its job without a chaperone. Phil glanced up. "You in the logs again?"

"Light monitoring," Matt said. "Post-holiday volumes are still weirdly high. Looks smooth."

Phil shook three sugar packets and tapped them twice on the counter. "Smooth is how you get complacent." He said, which sent a shiver down Matt's spine.

"What would you look at first?" Matt asked, trying and failing to keep his voice casual.

"Timestamp jitter," Phil said immediately. "Then routing delays, gateway slippage, decimal handling in the feed normalizer. People forget pennies are where the blood leaks out."

Pennies. The word landed like a tap on a glass. Matt nodded and excused himself, heart tapping back.

That evening, Matt hit the gym with a kind of fury he hadn't felt since college. Thirty minutes on the treadmill turned into forty-five. He punched up the incline, chased the lactic burn, and begged the noise in his head to convert into sweat.

By the time he got home, the sun was dropping; the kitchen was holding that soft golden light that forgives. He could smell seared steak coming from the apartment before he even rounded the corner. Bernice was at the stove, hair down in loose curls, wearing a summer dress in winter just because she could. A slim vase of red roses stood on the table. A bottle of Stag's Leap Artemis sweated in a bucket as if it had wandered in from a better life.

"What's this?" Matt asked, his voice catching around the edge of the room. She looked luminous.

"I know you're under some kind of stress," she said, laying a hand on his chest, reading the beat under her palm. "I want to help you relax."

"You didn't have to go all out."

"I wanted to." Her eyes lingered, searching him the way you read a familiar page to see what you missed last time.

Dinner was medium-rare sirloin with roasted garlic mash and grilled asparagus. They picked, letting the wine unpeel the tightness in the conversation. Guest lists, veto lists. Honeymoon daydreams: St. Lucia, Greece, Antigua, maybe Spain if they wanted to pretend their money went further than it did. Curtain colors for the townhouse. A dog someday. The ordinary future, easy to imagine when the food was good, and the light was kind, and the wine even better.

Eventually, the topic circled to money. Bernice mentioned her parents' offer to cover "most of it." Her voice was gentle, but the number hung there, anyway. "They want us to have a beautiful day," she said. "They've already started asking about venues."

Matt nodded, a dull knot forming. "Yeah. That's ... really kind."

"What about your folks? Think they'll be able to help a bit?"

He set down his fork. "They'll do what they can," he said. "But things are tight. They always have been."

Bernice reached across the table. "I get it. It's not about the money." She held his hand. "We're in this together."

He managed a smile. "I just wish I could do more. College was mostly loans. They've never really had savings."

"You already do more than enough."

For a stretch, he let her belief be true. The number in his head—$210.60—drifted to the back of his mind. Then, just as quickly, it was back.

He drifted mid-sentence. Bernice tilted her head. "Where'd you go just now?"

"Nowhere. Just tired."

She eased her hand back and folded her arms. "You're lying to me, Matt. I don't know what it is, but something's going on."

He froze. "It's work. I'm under pressure."

"No," she said, voice rising a notch. "It's more than that. You've been distant for weeks. You come home wired and then disappear into space. If it's not work, then what the hell is it?"

"I told you I'm under pressure!" The volume surprised them both. His chair scraped. "We're planning a wedding and arguing about money, and I feel like I'm failing at all of it."

"So do I!" she shot back, eyes wet now. "But I'm here, and you keep shutting me out."

He gripped the edge of the counter, knuckles blanching, the cool laminate grounding him and not letting go. "I didn't ask your parents for help. That's them. I wish my family could do more. It's humiliating."

Bernice held him with her eyes. Silence stretched. When she spoke again, her voice was lower. "I just need you to be honest with me. I'm not the enemy."

He turned. The fight leaked out of him as quickly as it had come. "I know you're not. I'm trying to hold it all together."

She stepped into him and wrapped her arms around his waist. He allowed her to hold him, and the tension changed from sharp to heavy. What followed in the bedroom was urgent and raw, less romance than release. Afterward, they lay tangled, breath syncing.

"Don't shut me out," she whispered into the hollow of his collarbone.

"I won't," he said. "I promise."

They lay there half-dressed for a while, then not dressed at all, and he finally slept like somebody had pulled the battery.

After midnight, he woke in the dark to the refrigerator's low hum and the heater's thin rattle. Bernice breathed evenly beside him. He slid out of bed like a thief and padded to the living room, toes finding the one loose board he always forgot about.

The laptop screen painted his face an icy blue. He logged in, opened terminal windows like shutters, and watched lines of life scroll by. Ten-cent fragments skimmed into the current and were gone, indistinguishable from the static.

He opened a notebook and wrote with a dull pencil:

Variance breathing?

Decimal handling, feed normalizer.

Phil: "Pennies are where the blood leaks out."

He checked the dummy account, closed it, and checked again as if the number might change if he stared hard enough.

It didn't.

He killed the screen and stood in the dark until his eyes picked out the outlines of their furniture, the couch, the slumped cardigan on its arm, the vase of roses now black shapes against the window. In the bathroom, he ran the tap and splashed water on his face until the cold made his teeth ache. Back in bed, he dreamed in columns of numbers that turned into falling coins, all ping and no weight.

Morning came too fast. He snoozed the alarm three times and woke with light already cutting through the blinds. No breakfast. Bernice handed him a travel mug and a kiss. "You're cutting it close," she said.

"I know. I'll make it up tonight."

He hit the parking lot at 9:12, jogged inside, and grabbed a refill from the break room. At his desk, he opened a terminal, hands not entirely steady, and rechecked the dummy account.

$401.90.

His fingers hovered over the mouse. The script was still running. No alerts. No noise.

He exhaled long and thin. It was no longer a theory.

It was a machine. And it was working.

CHAPTER 12
PANIC

The office was already humming by the time Matt arrived. Phones rang with their tinny, uneven trills. Keyboards clattered in syncopated bursts, some fast, some halting. The breakroom smelled of ever-present coffee, sausage biscuits, and the faint tang of microwaved egg sandwiches. On the surface, everything looked normal.

Matt hung his jacket on the back of his chair and tried to walk a measured circuit past ops. A few analysts glanced up from dual-monitor setups, their eyes glazed in spreadsheet focus. Someone offered him a quick "Morning, Matt." Another, a younger guy he barely knew, asked about wedding plans. "Nerves yet?" the guy said with a grin. Matt forced a smile, muttered something about colors and venues. Everyone looked relaxed. Nobody looked panicked. For one moment, he almost let himself breathe. But very quickly, his mind sprang back to the thrill he experienced by breaking the system.

Then, at 10:02 a.m., the email hit.

From: Rajive Singh
Subject: Development Staff; All Hands: Large Conference Room
Time: 10:15 a.m.

It landed like a bomb.

Matt's heart rate spiked. His vision pulsed. Impromptu meetings never carried good news, and the timing—just one day after he'd buried the ghost code and wiped the dummy account—felt cruelly precise. He had the sudden urgent urge to visit the bathroom.

He filed into the large conference room with all of the development team members. The blinds were closed, the overhead lights dimmed just enough to make everything feel clandestine. Nobody had set up the projector. No laptops, no slides. Just Rajive, standing at the head of the table in shirtsleeves, hands resting on the polished wood.

"Good morning," Rajive said, his voice calm, measured. "This won't take long. I wanted to let everyone know that the annual bonus process has officially begun."

The tension drained from Matt so fast it made him dizzy. He exhaled audibly, shoulders slumping. Ray caught the movement, raised an eyebrow, and smirked.

Rajive went on. "Team leads will make recommendations based on performance and contributions. I'll compile those for Richard. He'll make divisional calls. Final sign-off from Dennis. You'll all get your notifications within a week. Payouts will be part of March's check."

The room murmured with interest. A couple of developers cracked jokes about buying boats or retiring early. Chairs scraped lightly against the carpet as people shifted in relief.

Matt laughed with them, but inside, he felt as if he'd just walked away from a firing squad.

The rest of the morning blurred. He returned to his desk and stared at the lines of code that he had trouble reading. The relief was genuine, but fragile, like a sheet of thin ice letting the sunlight through. One loop of paranoia had closed. He knew another could open just as quickly.

At noon, Debbie How from HR invited him to her office for what she called a "check-in." The small room was windowless and painted a neutral beige that seemed designed to dull emotions. She had a neat stack of files, two sandwiches from the café down the street, and two cans of sparkling water on her desk.

"You've really settled in nicely," she said, unwrapping her turkey sandwich with precision. "Rajive tells me your transition's been seamless. Richard and Dennis have both noticed."

Matt picked at his roast beef on wheat, nodding. "That's good to hear. Still a lot to learn, but I'm enjoying it."

Debbie smiled, professional but warm. "We're impressed. Don't undersell yourself." She talked him through minor policy updates, PTO reminders, and open enrollment dates—nothing sharp, nothing dangerous.

He kept waiting for a shoe to drop, some probing question about logs or variances, but it never came. The conversation stayed trivial, almost comforting. He left her office lighter than he'd gone in.

Until 3:12 p.m.

Matt spotted Phil Morris walking across the floor, a manila folder tucked tight under his arm. Phil's long stride carried him straight to Dennis' office. Through the glass wall, Matt could see them: Phil pointing, flipping pages, Dennis leaning in, serious.

Fifteen minutes later, Phil left and headed straight for Richard Eastman, the CTO. Five minutes after that, Rajive was called in.

Matt's gut dropped—again. His skin went cold, damp.

He swiveled in his chair and opened a terminal. Fear made his fingers move before logic could stop them. He found the exact blocks of code he'd written—the siphon that had been hiding in Goose for weeks. His chest tightened as he highlighted every line. Delete. He switched to the database, pulled up the dummy account, and wiped it clean. Gone. Every trace.

He sat back, throat raw, eyes on the ceiling tiles. He mouthed a silent prayer, or maybe a plea for forgiveness.

Fifteen minutes later, Rajive appeared at their bullpen. "Guys," he said casually, "Phil spotted something weird this morning. A couple of accounts are showing minor discrepancies. Just a few dollars short, but he wants us to look."

Derek frowned. "How'd he catch it?"

"One of the daily accounting reports printed without a line total. He double-checked the raw data and found a mismatch. Just a couple of bucks, but it doesn't balance."

Ray leaned back. "Weird. That printing process hasn't glitched in years."

Matt's skin itched. His mouth tasted metallic, as if he'd bitten a coin. He said nothing.

The team got to work. Derek and Royland dove into reconciliation scripts, their muttered shorthand bouncing back and forth. Ray combed logs, tapping his pen against his teeth. Matt sat at his desk, queries open, but his brain was sludge. Every 10 minutes, he found an excuse to leave—bathroom, water, checking voicemail that didn't exist. His stomach flipped every time he passed Phil's office, the folder still sitting on the corner of his desk.

Two hours ticked by.

Finally, Derek leaned back, stretching his arms overhead. "Found it," he announced. "Currency conversion module. Edge case. When the report generator parsed values, it dropped a fractional cent. Not technically an error. Just rounding. Ugly but harmless."

Matt exhaled so hard he nearly coughed. Relief flooded him, but a strange aftertaste lingered. Derek's tone was too smooth, too practiced.

Derek summarized the findings for Rajive, who called Richard, who looped in Dennis. The group huddled, nodded, dispersed. The fire was out.

Derek walked back over. "Matt, can you draft a patch for the report engine? Nothing fancy. Just flag rounding gaps."

"Sure," Matt said. His voice cracked; he covered it with a cough.

Inside, he was already celebrating. It was over. He had brushed the edge of disaster and walked away untouched.

But as he watched Derek, calm and unruffled, the thought crept in: He's done this before. He knew exactly where to look. The doubt pierced sharper than relief. What if Matt wasn't the only one who'd seen how open the system really was?

That evening, Matt parked his Hyundai and walked into Marietta Square. The lamplight glowed soft amber; strings of bulbs crossed patios like low constellations. He was meeting Bernice and their friends, Clint and Maria, at Johnnie MacCracken's, the old firehouse-turned-pub that always smelled like stale beer.

Bernice was already there, perched at a high-top in dark jeans and a wine-colored blouse that made her eyes glow green. Her laugh carried across the room before her wave did.

They drank Guinness, passed around baskets of fried pickles, and traded stories. Bernice teased Matt about his color-coded wedding spreadsheet. Clint dramatized a disastrous bachelor party from his first marriage. Maria groaned and buried her face in her hands.

Matt tried to let himself sink into the warmth of it, the chatter, Bernice's effortless charm. She lit up the table, gesturing with her hands, making Clint roar with laughter one moment and offering Maria quiet sympathy the next when she mentioned a sick aunt.

Later at home, they lay in bed with the TV murmuring some cooking show in the background.

"Big day?" she asked.

"Yeah," Matt said. "We had a bonus meeting. Process is starting."

She perked up. "Any idea how much?"

"Rajive seems to imply, and Debbie confirmed that it would be in the region of 15 grand. But honestly, it's hard to know."

Bernice whistled. "Barcelona."

He grinned. "Barcelona."

She pulled out her laptop, scrolling through boutique hotels near the Gothic Quarter. "Spring would be perfect. Warm, not packed."

He wrapped his arm around her, eyes tracing the ceiling. For a moment, he let the fantasy wash over him.

Then Bernice's tone shifted. "Do you think there has been any change for your parents? Would they be able to put anything toward wedding costs?"

Matt stiffened. "A little, maybe. They want to. But flights and hotels will already stretch them. I don't want to push."

Bernice nodded slowly. "I get it. My parents are covering most of it. It just feels strange, like it's all on them."

"I know. I hate it too. It's not what I pictured."

"Maybe we should scale back."

Matt pulled her closer. "No. I want it perfect for you."

She smiled, but faintly. "I'd settle for not being stressed."

He kissed her forehead, but long after she fell asleep, he lay awake, staring into the dark. The code was gone. The account was gone.

But the risk, the thrill—those weren't gone at all.

And now, he hoped 15 thousand reasons would be enough to keep him from going back.

CHAPTER 13
VERSION 2

The next morning unfolded like clockwork. Matt and Bernice sat across from each other at their little kitchen table, sipping coffee and splitting a toasted bagel. The faint clink of knives on ceramic plates filled the air between them. Morning sun filtered through gauzy curtains, casting stripes of pale gold across the linoleum floor. Outside, the muffled sound of a garbage truck echoed down the street, mixing with the occasional bark of a neighbor's dog.

Bernice scrolled through news on her laptop, half-reading, with one elbow propped lazily on the table. Matt, distracted, stared at his mug, his mind running through lines of code like a chess player running through openings.

"You're awfully quiet today," she said, glancing at him over the rim of her coffee mug.

Matt looked up and managed a smile. "Just thinking through a bug I need to fix. One of those weird rounding issues."

She nodded, unconcerned. "That's why they pay you the big bucks."

He kissed her cheek before grabbing his jacket. "See you tonight."

He took his seat at his desk by 8:00 a.m. The office already buzzed with its usual morning rhythm: the whir of desktop fans, the rhythmic clatter of keyboards, and the clink of mugs against the chipped countertop in the breakroom.

Matt logged in, launched the application, and pulled up the codebase segment assigned to him. The official task: address the minor discrepancy Phil Morris had uncovered, the one everyone had already agreed was harmless.

But he knew there was nothing to fix.

Instead, he thought of his own skimming-script ghost, already erased from production but still alive in his head. His fingers hovered above the keyboard.

What if he brought it back—cleaner?

If he could weave in a reporting patch, the discrepancies wouldn't appear in printed audits. The system would look pristine. Balanced. *Clean.*

He leaned back in his chair, eyes flicking around the bullpen. Derek was muttering at his monitor; Ray and Royland were bickering about a front-end ticket. No one looked at Matt. He could have been invisible.

Two hours passed in near silence, broken only by the occasional shuffle of papers or cough from down the hall. During that time, Matt rewrote the code, line by line, building in safeguards, filters, and a camouflage routine. The new version intercepted reports before they hit the printer, subtly manipulating totals so the data matched what the accountants expected to see. It was elegant and untouchable.

He tested it against old datasets, his pulse racing with every query. It passed—every time.

Just before lunch, he rolled back his chair and stretched. "Patch is almost done," he said casually. "I'll probably push it tonight."

Royland looked up from his game of solitaire. "All good then?"

"Yeah," Matt said, keeping his voice even. "Should clean up the conversion rounding."

"Cool." Royland went back to his cards. Derek didn't even glance up, but said, "approved."

That evening, Matt stayed late. The Goose bullpen emptied by seven, the lights dimming automatically to half-brightness. By 8 p.m., he sat alone, accompanied only by the groan of the HVAC system. The emptiness was suffocating and liberating all at once.

He deployed the new code. First, the skimming script, refined and tempered. Then, the reporting patch. Finally, a tiny manual trigger script, tucked deep where no casual eye would ever find it.

For half an hour, he ran test queries, checked logs, and monitored for anomalies. Nothing. The screens glowed in perfect silence. He wasn't sure why he was doing it. It was certainly not for financial gain. But the thrill somehow engulfed him. Satisfied, he powered down, pulled on his jacket, and left the building.

Bernice was curled on the couch with her laptop when he walked in, a half-finished glass of wine beside her. She looked up, eyes warm.

"Hey," she said with a smile. "You look wiped."

"Long day," Matt murmured, dropping his bag by the door.

He sat beside her, wrapped an arm around her shoulders, and kissed her temple. Her warmth—her normalcy—grounded him. For a fleeting moment, everything felt safe.

The next morning, Matt was up before the sun.

He dressed quietly, skipped breakfast, and drove through streets still cloaked in the violet hush of dawn. Frost clung to windshields, glittering under streetlamps. His Hyundai's engine hummed in the silence as he pulled into the lot at 7:15.

Inside, the building was mostly dark. His footsteps echoed down the empty corridor as he keyed into the suite. Inside, he powered up his machine, opened a terminal, and ran the test script.

$101.30.

His pulse quickened. He exhaled slowly, checked the logs, and scanned the reports. All clean. The patch had masked the variance flawlessly. The totals balanced. Nothing flagged.

By the time the others arrived, Matt was already back in his seat, sipping coffee, the vague tremor in his hand invisible behind the mug.

"Patch is in," he said casually when Derek wandered by. "Looks stable."

"Great," Derek replied, without looking up.

Royland offered a thumbs-up. No one asked questions.

The rest of the day passed in a haze until 12:53 p.m. A calendar invite appeared in Matt's inbox:

Meeting: Bonus Confirmation.

Time: 1 p.m.

Attendees: Rajive Singh, Richard Eastman.

His stomach flipped.

At 1:00 p.m. sharp, Matt walked into the glass-walled conference room. Rajive and Richard had already sat down and were both smiling.

"Matt," Richard said warmly. "Close the door."

He did.

"We'll keep this short," Rajive began. "You're doing excellent work. We noticed the patch you put in earlier and the way you handled that reconciliation issue."

Richard leaned in. "You've been a great fit here. Smart, fast, and steady under pressure."

Matt's mouth was dry. He nodded mutely.

"We're awarding you a $45,000 bonus," Rajive said. "It'll hit your account next month."

Matt blinked. *Forty-five …*

"And," Richard added, "there may be a team lead role opening in the next quarter. You're at the top of the list."

Matt forced words out: "Wow ... that's ... incredible. Thank you. Really. I appreciate it."

"Well earned," Rajive said.

Back at his desk, Matt sat in a daze. The act that should have buried him had, instead, helped to elevate him. Money, recognition, opportunity, delivered on a silver platter. His hands shook faintly on the keyboard.

That night, over dinner at Bernice's favorite Italian bistro, he told her. The place glowed with a low amber light. Candles flickered in glass holders, the scent of garlic and tomatoes thick in the air. She wore a light blue wrap dress that turned heads.

"Forty-five grand?" She said, eyes wide. "Matt, that's ... unbelievable."

"I know. I didn't expect that much."

She clinked her wineglass against his. "Barcelona. Tonight, we book it."

Matt paused as he crossed his arms across his chest, deep in thought. He took a moment to temper the spinning gears.

"Better yet ..." he started, slowly, "with this much money at our disposal, we don't have to wait until after the wedding." He sat forward and clutched her hand across the table. "Bernie, I know this is sudden, but work's been stressful—for both of us. We need a break." Matt let go of her hand and leaned back in his chair, bracing for Benice's protests. "Let's do a trial run. Let's go this spring, make sure it's what we really want for our honeymoon."

"Matt ... that's ... big," Bernice said, leaning back herself. "I don't know if—"

"I don't know either," Matt interjected. "But I do know that I want to spend a sunny week in Spain with my beautiful fiancée, eating tapas and sipping cava. We deserve it. And now, we can afford it."

Bernice was having trouble finding reasons to say *no*. Matt had been so distant lately; maybe this "trial run" was exactly what they needed.

"You know what ... I think you might be right," Bernice said, grasping Matt's hand again. "Let's do it. Let's book it right now."

And they did. Her laptop open between them, scrolling through boutique hotels in the Gothic Quarter. Rooftop terraces. Tapas tours. Narrow cobblestone alleys lit with lanterns.

"Let's make it real," she said. "No laptops after dinner. Just us."

Matt smiled and agreed. She kissed him across the table.

Later that night, curled against him in bed, she whispered, "You're amazing, you know."

Matt stared at the ceiling. "Maybe," he whispered back with a fleeting smile.

But his chest was tight. Deep down, he knew he was lying— to her, to everyone. He told himself that it was still only a test. Someday, he would reveal the flaw and show them how easily they could break the system, that he was doing SBF a favor.

The words played in his head like a lullaby.

But they didn't soothe him. They only kept him awake.

CHAPTER 14
MOM

Though Matt had engineered the perfect system to skim money from incoming repayments within SBF, it was, at best, just an internal game. The code worked. The dummy account steadily grew. But the money, for now, lived only inside the company's ecosystem. It was unspendable, untouchable—a ghost balance with no door out.

The longer he stared at the dummy account, the more he realized that he hadn't solved the real problem. Extracting money from a closed-loop internal ledger without triggering compliance alarms was a completely distinct challenge.

One afternoon, Matt sat bored at his desk, his mind wandering as the team debugged an underwriting module. He leaned back in his chair, eyes drifting up toward the buzzing lights above. The ceiling vent rattled faintly, spilling cold air across his neck. He closed his eyes and asked himself: *How would an actual thief get the money out?*

It wasn't as simple as opening a bank account. Know Your Customer and Office of Foreign Assets Control regulations meant that every account opening left fingerprints. He couldn't just walk into a bank in the US and open an account without using his own identity. Even if he could redirect funds to an external bank, getting access without leaving a trail back to himself would be nearly impossible.

Matt played with the idea for days. Then weeks.

He turned it over during his treadmill runs at the gym, during long coding lulls, even while lying awake beside Bernice as she breathed softly into the night.

The solution had to exist because this was no longer a technical problem. He knew he could solve the technical piece. This was architectural, almost philosophical.

Eventually, he landed on the only genuine answer: he'd have to move the money to a jurisdiction where American oversight didn't reach. Somewhere with loose banking controls, little appetite for international cooperation, and barely functioning compliance departments.

After weeks of research, reading obscure financial blogs, scrolling through forums, and opening VPN-masked browser sessions late at night, he narrowed the field.

The Caribbean.

Specifically, a small, unregulated island bank with minimal KYC standards. It would need to offer remote account opening, digital access, and, most importantly, no reporting back to the US authorities.

He had even found one: Commonwealth Trust Bank, a three-branch operation based in Antigua, privately owned and operating outside the FATCA jurisdiction.

Just weeks before their vacation to Spain, Matt was deep into vetting the bank's application forms and cross-referencing travel restrictions when his phone rang.

The caller ID indicated it was Clare.

His sister never called.

"Hey," he answered quickly. "Everything okay?"

Her voice was shaky. "It's Mom. She's in the hospital. I don't know exactly what's wrong, but she's in a lot of pain. Something with her stomach. They're running tests."

Matt shot up from his chair, already reaching for his laptop with his free hand. "I'm booking a flight now. I'll be there tonight."

"Are you sure? It might not—"

"I'm coming. Text me the hospital name."

He called Bernice immediately. She was at work. He could hear the muted office clatter in the background.

"I just got off the phone with Clare. My mom's in the hospital."

"Oh no," Bernice said. "Do you want me to come with you?"

He hesitated, heart thudding. "Not yet. I'll get down there and figure out what's going on first."

She paused. "Okay. Let me know how I can help."

Her tone was warm but edged with understandable concern as they said their goodbyes.

Matt walked over to Derek's desk and explained. Derek, always gruff but surprisingly compassionate, told him to take all the time he needed, but to let Rajive know.

Rajive echoed the same. "Family comes first," he said. "Keep us updated."

As Matt was logging off and packing up his laptop, Dennis passed by, eyes sharp.

"Everything okay?" Dennis asked, glancing at the monitor.

"Family emergency," Matt said. "My mom."

Dennis nodded slowly. "Safe travels. Keep us posted."

Matt walked out thinking, *God, nothing gets past that guy.*

He arrived in Bay Ridge just past midnight. The cab ride from JFK was silent except for the hiss of tires on wet asphalt. The city looked half asleep, Christmas lights still strung across stoops, trash bags stacked neatly against brownstones.

His mind bounced between dread and exhaustion, Antigua and family colliding in his head. Clare met him at the hospital entrance, eyes shadowed with fatigue. Together, they rode the elevator to the fifth floor of NYU Langone Hospital in Brooklyn.

His mother lay in a dim room, tubes in her arm, monitors softly beeping. The antiseptic tang of disinfectant clung to the air. She looked pale, but lucid.

"Matthew," she said with a weak smile. "You didn't need to come all this way."

He bent down and kissed her forehead. "Yes, I did."

His father sat in the corner, looking drained, shoulders slumped forward in his chair. "They don't know exactly what it is yet," he said. "Something with the intestines. They're doing more scans in the morning."

Matt stayed the night on an awkward vinyl recliner, but sleep never arrived. The noises of the hospital kept him awake —the soft whoosh of ventilators, the squeak of nurses' shoes on tile, the distant ring of a phone. Yet, the background din was only part of it; he was also flushed with guilt. He hadn't seen his parents for nearly a year, and even now, with his mother hospitalized, his mind drifted toward Antigua. Toward Commonwealth Bank. The phantom balance was still swelling inside SBF's ledger.

The next morning, the doctors came in with answers. They found a mass in her lower intestine. It wasn't conclusive yet, but they suspected it was benign. The doctors scheduled the surgery for the following day.

Matt texted Bernice the update. She offered to fly in that afternoon. He told her to wait, just in case things took a turn.

That evening, he called her again. Their trial run to Spain was just days away.

"We have to cancel," he said.

There was a long silence on the line.

"Okay," Bernice said. "Let's look at the insurance paperwork. I'm pretty sure we're covered. We can always rebook."

"You're amazing, you know that?"

"I do," she said, her voice light but steady. "But keep saying it."

The surgery went well. The doctors removed the mass cleanly and confirmed post-op that it wasn't cancerous. Her recovery would take several weeks, but she'd be okay.

Matt stayed for a few more days. The smell of carrots and thyme filled his parents' cramped kitchen as he made soup to bring to the hospital. He picked up prescriptions from the corner pharmacy, the bag crinkling in his hand. He walked the long, quiet streets of Bay Ridge with his dad, past shuttered diners and corner bodegas. They talked about nothing—and everything. Still, a quiet distance sat between them. His father hadn't said it, but Matt could sense it: the life he'd built in Georgia felt further away than ever.

One night, as the sun set behind the Verrazzano Bridge, Matt found himself standing alone at the water's edge. His mother's prognosis was good. He should have felt relief. Yet, his mind surged forward, past recovery, past family, toward a narrow side street in St. John's, where the glass front doors of Commonwealth Trust Bank stood vivid in his imagination.

He could picture it all: a fake name. A PO box. A VPN masked his logins. The transfer mechanism was still unclear, but he was close. Certain.

His mom left the hospital a day later. Matt made sure she was comfortable, stocked the fridge, and left his number on a Post-it Note even though everyone already had it. He booked a flight back to Atlanta for the next day.

That final night, lying in his childhood bed beneath posters of long-faded bands and peeling wallpaper, he stared at the ceiling, heartbeat slow and steady, thinking of the code still buried inside Goose. That was it: a half-completed challenge. A ghost balance.

He told himself again that it was all just a test—a demonstration.

CHAPTER 15
ANTIGUA PLAN

Matt flew back to Atlanta late the next day and drove straight from the airport to their townhouse. The porch light was on, casting a warm glow across the front steps, and Bernice was waiting, arms crossed against the chill. The second he stepped through the door, she wrapped her arms around him and held on longer than usual.

"You smell like hospitals," she murmured into his shoulder.

"Sorry," he said, hugging her tightly. "It's been a rough few days."

Inside, Matt was quickly comforted, savoring the scents of lavender candles and lemon cleaner. After unpacking and showering off the hospital smell and airplane grime, Matt joined Bernice in the living room. The couch was soft; the throw blanket draped over the back still carried her perfume. They poured two glasses of red wine and curled up together, the quiet ticking of the wall clock filling the spaces between words.

Matt opened up about his mother's condition, the surgery, and the emotional weight of being back home. Bernice listened intently, nodding, her hand resting gently on his knee. She didn't interrupt. She never did.

When he finally paused, she kissed him softly and said, "Don't worry about the vacation; I already submitted the insurance claim. We'll get the money back."

Matt smiled, the corners of his mouth tightening with both gratitude and guilt. "Thank you."

"Should we make a plan to rebook the trip to Barcelona?"

He hesitated. The thought of a nine-hour flight to Europe suddenly felt oppressive. Endless lines, too many people, too much exposure. And more than anything, too many eyes. What he told Bernice was true: he wanted to relax. But it wasn't the whole truth. Deep inside, something else had taken root: a quiet calculation. Antigua wasn't just closer. It was strategically convenient.

Caribbean islands, particularly the smaller ones, continued to emerge during his research into offshore jurisdictions with lax banking regulations. He hadn't planned it this way, but now that the idea had planted itself, he couldn't ignore it. He wasn't planning to open an account, at least not yet. But if the opportunity presented itself, if he could do it without raising suspicion, wouldn't it make sense to be prepared?

"I've been thinking," he said slowly. "Maybe we'll go somewhere closer. Caribbean, maybe. Antigua?"

Bernice blinked. "Antigua? What about Spain?" Bernice paused to collect herself. "I've been dreaming about this trip for months—Barcelona, Gaudí, the tapas crawl. We ruled out the Caribbean ages ago ..."

"I just ... I don't want to spend an entire day at airports," he said carefully. "And I feel like we need something more relaxing. White sand, turquoise water. Something *easy*."

She tilted her head, narrowing her eyes. "You sure this isn't about something else? Because this feels sudden, Matt. I mean, Barcelona's been our trial-run plan for months. We already planned the hotels, the food tours, and the walking tours. You were the one who pushed for this. What happened to all that?"

He gave a weak smile, then sighed. "I know it seems sudden. It's just ... after everything with Mom, and sitting in that hospital room for days, it made me realize how drained I really am. The idea of airports and long flights and nonstop touring just feels ... exhausting right now. I want something quiet, something simple."

They debated over another glass of wine, voices rising and softening like waves against a jetty. Bernice was caught off guard but didn't push too hard, and Matt did his best to put her mind at ease.

After an hour, she had warmed to the idea. She pulled her laptop onto her lap, the blue glow lighting her face, and together they scrolled through resort options.

They settled on St. John's Resort in Antigua: an all-inclusive, beachfront suite. A far cry from their original plans to explore Catalan architecture and tapas bars, but it felt right for the moment, and to make things even better, it turned out to be cheaper.

"I can already feel the sun on my skin," Bernice mused, eyes twinkling as she tapped the final booking confirmation for that summer.

But Matt wasn't finished planning. That night, he couldn't sleep. While Bernice lay beside him, lightly snoring, he turned over and stared at the ceiling. The white noise of the air conditioning hummed faintly, and outside, the bark of a neighbor's dog cut through the silence.

In his mind, Matt began to rehearse what opening an offshore account would look like. He considered the questions they might pose. The documents they might require. The stories he might need to tell. He pictured himself in a collared shirt, clipboard in hand, sitting across from some middle-aged clerk in a brightly lit, sparsely decorated office at Commonwealth Trust Bank of Antigua, trying to look like a confused but earnest American tourist.

He imagined walking on the beach the morning of the appointment, hand in hand with Bernice, while rehearsing cover stories in his head. Something about setting up a wedding gift account. Maybe a small investment vehicle. Something vague and boring.

When sleep finally came, it was restless and unrewarding.

The next morning, Bernice mentioned looking into snorkeling excursions and sunset catamaran cruises. Matt nodded, distracted. His thoughts were already miles away, deep in the Caribbean, buried under layers of encryption and secrecy.

Soon, Matt was back at work. On the surface, nothing had changed. The buzz of fluorescent lights, the faint, constant whir of the cooling systems above, the burble of coffee pots in the pantry. Phones chirped, keyboards clattered, and somewhere down the hall, a printer jammed with its usual sigh.

It was business as usual. But for Matt, everything was shifting.

After his experience in New York and the emotional whirlwind of canceling a dream vacation, he found himself more numb than ever at work. Even the monotony didn't irritate him the same way; it simply blurred into the background like static. Still, to keep his mind busy, he returned to his concealed project—his challenge.

During breaks, he began sketching out code that could siphon funds from the dummy account to send them externally. Not just an internal hidden skim, but actual movement. Real extraction.

The challenge consumed him. He started logging into the system through a shadow shell, reviewing access logs twice a day. Every harmless comment from Derek felt loaded. Every time Royland walked by his desk, Matt resisted the urge to minimize his windows.

It had to be undetectable. It had to be bulletproof. And above all, it had to leave no trail. He wasn't stealing. He was never planning on taking any money for himself. He was still just exploring the potential, set on exposing the system's weaknesses—that was it.

By Thursday, he had a script that, when executed, would move small amounts every few days from the dummy account to a new destination. But he had no such destination. No bank account. No place to send the money. Testing it wasn't even an option. But Antigua would be the answer. He labeled the new script Bailer—a quiet, maybe even subconscious, nod to what it might one day help him do.

Matt realized he was searching for something else now, something more abstract than wealth, more challenging than peace of mind.

He wanted proof.

Proof that he could see the loophole others missed, build something from nothing, outsmart a system designed to be foolproof, and, in his mind, save SBF from self-destructing.

The skimming challenge and the trip to Antigua weren't about money; they were about curiosity. About possibility. A private test and personal challenge. A quiet engineering puzzle cloaked in palm trees and ocean spray.

In his mind, it was still just an exercise, a detour through the mechanics of deception, not the act itself.

And that's what this had become: not a simple lone of code or an ordinary vacation, but a sandbox for the mind of a man who wasn't ready to admit what he was really building. Should he succeed, he would prove he could beat the system, revealing the man behind the curtain to be sharper than the rest.

It was all harmless, he kept telling himself.

CHAPTER 16
FIRST NIGHT IN PARADISE

After Matt had returned from New York, life had settled into a rhythm that, from the outside, looked enviable. His mother was recovering well, better than expected, and now called him every Sunday with cheerful updates. Work at SBF had returned to its usual drone of quiet efficiency: competent colleagues, minimal pressure, and little challenge. The boredom had crept back in.

At home, though, things were more complicated. His relationship with Bernice had deepened in some ways. They cooked together, planned their wedding for July of the following year, and spent long evenings half-watching TV, half-dreaming aloud. But there were tensions too. Money was tight. They hadn't expected to be asked to help with his mother's medical bills. This had stretched their savings thin, and the delay in the townhouse construction meant more rent payments toward their cramped apartment. Bernice had started tracking their expenses anxiously. Matt avoided the spreadsheets.

They rarely argued, but the air felt different lately, heavier, more brittle. A conversation about their new honeymoon destination had turned into a standoff, then a sulk, then a silent truce, then make-up sex. Antigua had started as a compromise. Now, it felt like a test.

On the evening before their departure, their small apartment looked like a particularly fashion-forward burglar had ransacked it. Clothes everywhere. Flip-flops, bathing suits, guidebooks dog-eared at glossy photos of beaches. Hair ties knotted around brushes. A lone pair of sunglasses perched on a stack of mail like a judge about to issue a ruling.

Matt zipped and unzipped the same suitcase twice, the motion mechanical. Beneath the vacation buzz wove a darker thread: what would it take to move the money, truly move it? This wasn't a test anymore. It was inertia turning into intent.

The next morning, their apartment was still in chaos. The comforter was a staging ground; the floor, a second suitcase. Matt double-checked zippers: Bernice shouted over the hair dryer.

"Did you pack the sunscreen?"

"Yes! Bottom of the left bag!"

"And the passports?"

Matt froze. "I thought you had them."

Bernice stuck her head out of the bathroom, face pale. "You're joking."

Matt broke into a grin and held up the small leather case with a dramatic flourish. "Gotcha." The tension in her voice had been real. For a moment, he hated himself for enjoying the joke.

"Asshole," she muttered, laughing as she vanished back into the fog of hairspray. "You're buying airport coffee."

Fifteen minutes later, they locked the door and wheeled their bags down the echoing hallway. The driver, a stocky man with tired eyes and a Braves cap, smelled faintly of cigarette smoke and cologne that had outlasted three fares. He hoisted the luggage with a grunt and swung the sedan into the slow river of traffic.

"Still no news about the townhouse?" Matt asked as the skyline slid past like cardboard cutouts in a diorama.

Bernice sighed. "I called the builder again this morning. They say late September now. Framing got delayed because of the rain."

"That's three months behind schedule."

"And three more months of rent," she said, thumb tapping at an invisible calculator on her thigh. "I was picturing dinner on the deck by now."

"Instead, we're still sharing walls with the two lovebirds next door. Mr. Loud TV and Mrs. Garlic Everything."

She laughed and nudged him. "One day we'll laugh about this."

"Today is not that day."

Hartsfield-Jackson was its usual choreography of rolling suitcases, announcements, and harried families. They split a limp airport burger and fries at a high-top under a fluorescent halo. The bar TV showed a looping weather map no one watched.

"Five bucks for a Bud Light?" Matt muttered, studying the receipt.

They boarded the 6:30 p.m. flight, still grumbling about the overpriced food, and found their seats amid the rustle of magazines and seatbelts. As the plane lifted and the cabin lights dimmed, Bernice laced her fingers through his, a slight squeeze like a quiet vow.

"We're really doing this," she whispered. The overhead dimmers threw a soft glow across her cheek. For a moment, Matt saw a future they'd both sold each other: carefree, sun-drenched, simple. Beneath it, the old weight shifted: cost, guilt, and a secret idea that had stopped being hypothetical.

He squeezed back. *Promise me*, he thought. *Promise us.*

The flight was uneventful, three hours measured in plastic cups and the soft hiss of the air nozzles. A flight attendant joked about island time; a toddler two rows back chatted in singsong about clouds. They dozed in shifts, shoulder to shoulder.

They descended through a blanket of Caribbean clouds and touched down at V.C. Bird International a little after 9:45 p.m. The heat met them on the jet bridge, a soft, wet hand to the chest. Outside, the night air was heavy, humid, and layered with the smell of salt and hibiscus.

Immigration was slow but cheerful. A short-sleeved officer stamped their passports and asked, "Honeymoon?"

Bernice smiled, then glanced at Matt. "Something like that …"

They quickly walked through the customs hall, which smelled vaguely of floor wax. When they emerged, a driver waited beneath a sodium lamp with a cardboard sign: ST. JOHN'S RESORT HALL.

He loaded their bags into a battered white van, its dashboard decorated with a small rosary and a bobblehead that nodded at every pothole. The roads were narrow; the asphalt was patched like quilt squares. They passed breezy, pastel houses with corrugated roofs and porches lit by single bulbs, dogs patrolling fences with sleepy authority. Somewhere, bass thumped through the dark, felt more than heard. Palms leaned over the road, listening to each passerby.

St. John's Resort opened from the dark like a stage set. The lobby was grand, open-air, and candlelit, with polished stone floors that glowed in the low light. A ceiling fan turned slowly. A woman at the desk presented cool towels and two glasses of rum punch.

"I apologize," the receptionist quietly interjected, "but your original room is currently unavailable. Nothing serious, just a broken AC. As a gesture of apology for the inconvenience, we have upgraded you to a honeymoon suite—no extra charge."

Bernice took a sip and giggled. "How fitting ... I think I love it here already."

A porter guided them along a winding stone path framed by hibiscus and low bougainvillea, crickets sawing in a steady rhythm. The sea was a presence even in the dark, close, breathing. Their casita was a single-story stucco under a red-tile roof, with a warm amber glow behind gauzy curtains. Sand had collected in crescent moons along the path.

Inside, the room was cool, with polished floors and French doors ajar to the terrace. An ornate king bed rested under delicate mosquito netting draped like a veil. A small carved table sat just beside the bed, topped with a humble bowl of fruit: bananas, grapefruits, and two small mangoes. The AC hummed just loud enough to be comforting.

Matt dropped the bags by the armoire and sat on the edge of the bed. "We're not supposed to be somewhere this nice," he said, more to the room than to Bernice. He felt as if they were walking into a life tailored for someone else's wallet, hoping not to set off alarms.

"Our dreamy honeymoon suite ..." Bernice said, turning slowly, taking it all in. The last of her Barcelona disappointment flickered, then softened. "I couldn't have imagined anything better."

"It's a practice run," Matt said with a grin. "Well, a practice run for our future rich, married selves."

"I feel like a fraud," Bernice joked, but the word knocked against something deep in Matt. "Let's just enjoy the spontaneity of it all. I am proud of us." She gently kissed his forehead.

They unpacked in slow motion: sundresses folded into drawers, polo shirts lined up with pointless precision, sandals kicked neatly under the bench. Bernice misted her face with rosewater; Matt cracked two minibar waters, the lids snapping like tiny promises. He noticed how the AC shivered the curtains and how quickly the bottles sweated in the heat.

"Want to check out the bar for a nightcap?" She asked, sliding into sandals, hair softly floating against her shoulders.

The walk took two minutes: a moonlit path, sand whispering underfoot, the low hush of waves growing louder. The bar was a thatched-roof pavilion with string lights braided along beams and a view of the pool that looked like poured mercury. A duo tapped out slow, melodic steel-drum tunes. The bartender in a crisp white shirt grinned as they slid onto stools.

"First night?" he asked.

"Just arrived," Matt said.

"Then you start with the house cocktail: *Trust Me Punch*."

Two tall glasses appeared in seconds, garnished with pineapple spears and neon straws. The ice clinked like glass bells. Bernice leaned against Matt, her shoulder warm against his arm.

"Everything's perfect," she said.

Matt nodded, eyes roaming the soft-lit grounds. He cataloged small things—the squeak of a loose fan blade above the bar, the bite of chlorine that lifted each time the wind shifted, the way the pool lights threw shifting, glowing scales across the ceiling. It felt like a movie set they'd snuck into.

A flicker of guilt intruded: Derek's offhand joke last week about a "surprise audit," delivered with a tone that hadn't sounded entirely like a joke. The thought passed like a shadow across a window.

"Ready to head back?" Bernice murmured after a few sips, already softened by travel and rum.

They walked hand in hand; the path dappled with moonlight and the occasional rustle in the shrubs. The tide had come in; the waves down the beach were louder, more insistent. The air smelled of salt and frangipani. In the room, Bernice disappeared into the bathroom. Water ran. A cabinet door clicked. Matt stepped onto the terrace.

The sea was a dark sheet, the horizon a thin seam that felt imagined. A breeze pressed against his chest and slid away. He could feel the pull of the plan, the way a current takes your ankles if you stand too long. Last-mile steps. Clean sessions. IP masks. An exit path that left no prints.

Bernice emerged in a tank top and lace underwear, hair loose, mouth soft with rum. She leaned against him on the terrace, cool tile under their bare feet.

"This place is magic," she said.

"You're magic," he replied, and kissed her. He could taste the sugar in the punch and the salt in the air.

What followed was unhurried and familiar, the intimacy that belongs to people who truly know each other. The heat made everything slower, heavier. Sheets clung. Laughter surfaced and sank again. They gulped water from sweating bottles, then found each other again, easy as breathing.

Afterward, they lay tangled under the netting, the ceiling fan slicing the air into lazy spirals. Bernice's fingers drew small circles on his chest.

"We're lucky," she murmured, already half asleep. "To have this. To have each other."

Matt watched as the curtain lifted and fell in the doorway, its fabric breathing in time with the surf. He counted the seconds between sets the way he counted intervals in code. How soon could he slip out for a walk that looked like a walk? How clean could he keep his trail? He had to find the perfect time, knowing the island had its own clock. He would obey it for now.

"Yeah," he said finally, kissing her bare shoulder.

He rolled onto his back and let the fan's slow cadence settle in his bones. Outside, the waves kept rolling. Somewhere down the beach, a late laugh rippled, then nothing but the hush. The island exhaled. The room cooled by degrees.

For the first time in months, Matt felt still, held between the life he shared with Bernice and the secret he was already weaving into something permanent. Curiosity, he'd tell himself again, an engineer's sandbox in palm trees. He'd tell himself he wasn't stealing. He'd tell himself he could stop.

Sleep came in shallow swells, and each time he surfaced, he heard the ocean and believed, for a breath or two, that the lulling sound was enough to calm the tumult within.

By morning, the stillness would break. The day would bring sun on the water and an unfamiliar edge to his thoughts. But for that first night, paradise held.

CHAPTER 17
SEED

They finally fell asleep at about 1 a.m. They had taken a brief walk around the resort on the way to the bar the night before, but by the next morning, the island truly revealed itself. Everything was better than the pictures.

Beyond their terrace, the water was impossibly blue, calm, and clear. Matt stood shirtless near the railing, a coffee in hand, watching the slow sway of the palm trees.

"You okay?" Bernice called from inside.

"Just taking it in," he said. "This place is unreal."

They spent most of Saturday at the beach. Yet even as Matt stretched out beside Bernice, his mind strayed to the folder he'd hidden away in his bag, the one with papers he hadn't admitted to bringing.

The secret weight of it gave the turquoise water and perfect sky an odd edge, as though the beauty of the place demanded more than relaxation, more than swimming, lounging, and reading.

The resort was quiet, adults-only, and catered to couples who didn't want crowds. Service arrived by gentle interruption, a smiling attendant with cold towels, cocktails, or fruit skewers. Lunch was grilled mahi-mahi with papaya salsa.

By midafternoon, they had already stopped checking the time. Both of them felt boozy, and Bernice suggested going back to the suite for a nap. After an hour locked in deep sleep and a further hour embraced in passion, they showered and readied themselves for a night out.

Dinner was at the open-air restaurant, perched slightly above the beach. They sat under a thatched awning; hurricane lanterns softly lit the table. Bernice wore a simple white sundress and no makeup. She looked like a postcard.

"Remind me why we shouldn't do this every year?" She asked, sipping her wine.

Matt smiled. "Because we live in a box above a parking lot and will soon have a mortgage to pay."

"Hey, that's our box," she mused. "Don't knock it." They laughed, clinked glasses, and watched the moonlight ripple on the water.

"But don't forget," Matt said, holding Benice's hand, "if we want, we *can* come back here next summer—for our *actual* honeymoon."

"There is no way I could say *no* to that," Benice said, as they both giggled again, already feeling like newlyweds.

But beneath the laughter, Matt's thoughts continued to tug elsewhere. He told himself the hidden folder in his bag was only a precaution, a just-in-case notion. Yet here, with the moonlight on the waves, the idea carried a gravity of its own, an itch he couldn't ignore, a plan already beginning to take shape.

———

SUNDAY DRIFTED by like a warm breeze. They had woken late, made love, and strolled barefoot to breakfast. The restaurant served thick banana pancakes and fresh guava juice. Matt drank strong coffee while Bernice read a paperback she'd picked up at the airport.

In the afternoon, they took a paddleboard out into the cove, where sea turtles bobbed in the shallows. Bernice sang 90s pop songs off-key. Matt pretended to paddle harder to escape. Yet, even there, he couldn't escape the pull of the folder.

That night's dinner was a bit more formal, jackets optional, seafood tower recommended. They were seated at a corner table just above the beach, the flicker of candlelight dancing across Bernice's collarbone.

"This place ..." she said dreamily, her second glass of wine half-finished. "It's like being inside a screensaver."

Matt smiled. "Yeah."

"You ever think about just ... saying screw it and moving somewhere like this?" she asked, almost joking.

Matt didn't answer immediately. He swirled the wine in his glass and watched the reflection of the moon flicker inside it. "Actually, yes," he said at last. "More and more lately."

She blinked, surprised. "Really? I was kind of kidding."

"I'm not. Not really. I mean, think about it; how hard would it be, really? People do it all the time. We could rent out the townhouse once we have purchased it, downsize to a small place here, and figure things out."

Bernice tilted her head, narrowing her eyes.

Part of her was thrilled at the fantasy—escape, calm beauty, mornings by the sea.

But another part tallied the realities: the townhouse purchase waiting back home, student loans still heavy, the weighty responsibilities she carried.

"Are you saying that as if you've thought it through before?" She asked, half curious, half uneasy, trying to decide whether this was playful banter or something far more serious.

Matt responded, grinning, "Maybe. Maybe I have a spreadsheet. Maybe I've calculated how far a modest consulting income would go in Antigua."

She laughed, but there was a softness in it. "You're nuts."

"Am I? You know you've felt it too. This place gets into your bones."

"Okay. Just hypothetically. If we ever did something like that ... I'd want a place with shutters. The kind that clap in the wind and let the morning light through." Bernice smiled. "And a porch. Definitely a porch. And maybe a hammock. For wine naps."

Matt nodded, letting the moment bloom between them.

"Exactly," he said. "No timeline. No pressure. Just something we could aim toward. A marker on the horizon."

She leaned in, touched her glass to his. "To someday."

"To someday."

She reached for his hand across the table. "It's a lovely thought."

They talked little after that. Just lingered over dessert and watched the waves roll in. And while Bernice let herself drift on the romance of the moment, Matt felt the quiet throb of his hidden plan, the folder in his bag calling to him even as the candles burned low.

The secret made the night feel sharper, more electric, as if the waves themselves were keeping his confidence. Something had been planted. But something else had already taken root—something Matt hadn't yet named.

MONDAY MORNING BROUGHT RESTLESS ENERGY. From the hotel desk, they rented a beat-up Suzuki with a manual transmission and optional AC, and quickly set off to explore the island. Bernice navigated with a cartoonish, fold-out map provided by the concierge. They drove south along the coast, past sugarcane fields and low stone churches, then cut inland through winding roads shaded by mahogany trees.

Matt slowed as they passed a hand-painted sign nailed to a fence:

Cottage for Sale, Sea View, Enquire Within.

Bernice leaned toward the window. "Oh, look at that one." The cottage was simple, but heartbreakingly beautiful in its setting. Stucco walls, the color of old yellow parchment flaked in the sun, and faded turquoise shutters hung slightly askew on salt-rusted hinges. A wide porch ran the length of the front, shaded by the overhang of a corrugated tin roof that glinted silver under the Caribbean light. The sea spread out beyond the front lawn like a never-ending pane of glass, azure in the center, cobalt where the reef broke the tide. Bougainvillea spilled over one side of the porch, and wild grass danced in the breeze as if it had a rhythm of its own. It looked forgotten, a little wounded, but undeniably alive. The kind of place that didn't ask for improvement, only company.

"That's the one," Matt said. "You wake up there, you never go back."

She laughed but initially said nothing.

Then, after a beat, she said, "Should we stop?"

Matt glanced over. "You want to?" She was already unbuckling her seatbelt. "We're on vacation. We can do what we want."

He pulled the car over onto a patch of gravel, and they stepped out into the heat. The scent of sunbaked grass and sea air wrapped around them. A narrow path led from the road to the porch. They didn't go inside. There was no sign of an agent, but they wandered around the front yard, peered through the salt-streaked windows, and stood together at the edge of the porch, gazing out toward the sea.

"Tell me you couldn't imagine it," Matt said softly.

Bernice exhaled. Her mind tumbled. She could see herself

here, shutters rattling in the wind, mornings scented with salt. But the thought of leaping terrified her. Back home, bills waited, family expectations pressed, and the townhouse contract loomed. "I can. That's what scares me." They stood there for a while, silent, then turned and walked back to the car.

They stopped for lunch at a roadside shack overlooking a bay. They had grilled snapper, rum punch, and a view of anchored sailboats bobbing in the cove.

"You were serious last night, weren't you?" Bernice asked.

Matt paused. "Yeah. I think I was."

She stirred her drink. "It's tempting. But we have real life to get back to. Family. Work. The townhouse."

"Of course. But what if we just ... planned for it? Not now, not even next year. Just made it part of the map."

She looked at him with something between curiosity and caution. "Yeah, maybe ..."

They drove back in silence, hand in hand, watching the ocean to their right.

AS TUESDAY MORNING BLOOMED, the light seeped lazily through the linen drapes. Bernice was already stretching, with a towel wrapped around her chest. "Spa day," she said, smiling. "I'll be gone until at least four. You going to be okay by yourself?"

Matt nodded, still beneath the covers.

"I might write. Or nap. Or just stare at the sea ..." He paused. "I did have a thought, though. What if we opened a savings account down here? Nothing big, just a *someday* fund. Maybe for our future little yellow cottage. I could make the arrangements today."

"If that will get us closer to that cottage, I say go for it." She kissed him and started toward the bathroom. "But really, just a small first deposit," she called over her shoulder. "We won't have much extra after this trip."

Once she left, he sat up, pulled on a T-shirt, and retrieved the looming folder. Inside were the details of a Delaware company. He wasted no time. By 9:30, he had signed on to his laptop and placed the order, submitted the basic form, and paid by credit card. Square Consulting LLC was born. He typed out a brief note to the resort's front desk:

Hi there, would it be possible to print a few forms for me?

I'll email them over.

Nothing urgent. Thank you.

He attached the articles of organization, a simple letterhead invoice template, and a cover note addressed to Commonwealth Trust Bank of Antigua. Then he slipped on his sandals, walked down the stone path to the lobby, and asked if the papers had come through. They had. The concierge handed them over with a smile.

By noon, he was in a cab headed into St. John's. The capital was alive with sound and color. Street vendors shouted, reggae pulsed from storefronts, and the scent of jerk chicken drifted through the heavy air.

Matt clutched the folder in his lap, sweating through his shirt, heart thudding. The bank was three blocks from the cathedral, with whitewashed walls, green shutters, and a brass plaque that simply read:

Commonwealth Trust Bank of Antigua.

Inside, it was cool, quiet, and orderly. A receptionist glanced up.

"Can I help you, sir?"

"Yes, thank you. I'd like to open a corporate account," he said. "For a newly registered US business."

She nodded and gestured to a chair. "Please fill out this form, and someone will be right with you."

He sat, pen shaking slightly as he filled out the lines. Name. Business type. Registered agent. Nature of services. A tall woman in a gray blouse and wire-rim glasses appeared 10 minutes later, her expression unreadable.

"Mr. Hall? Please come with me," she said, her island accent clipped, formal, and carrying just enough edge to make Matt's stomach tighten as he rose to follow.

The back office was modest but neat. A small desk, an old printer, and a ticking clock. She introduced herself as Andrea. Her voice was calm, neutral. She flipped through his paperwork, asked polite questions, and typed something into a terminal. "You'll need a minimum opening deposit of 1,000 US dollars. Are you prepared to wire that today?"

"Not today, but as soon as I get back home to the US," Matt said, then hesitated as Andrea looked up from her terminal. "The account will only officially be opened when it's been funded," she said.

Matt nodded.

She tilted her head slightly. "Mr. Hall, we will also need two forms of identification—a passport and a driver's license, and a recent utility bill or lease agreement to verify your address. These are standard requirements."

Matt's mouth went dry. "Of course. I expected that." From the folder, he slid forward a pair of fabricated consulting invoices he had created on Square Consulting letterhead. "I also brought supporting documents from my US business, proof of active work."

Andrea's gaze sharpened. She examined the invoices, her fingers brushing the ink as if to test its authenticity. Then she looked back up. "And your second form of ID?" Matt reached for his wallet, produced his Georgia driver's license, and tried to look casual as her eyes flicked between the card and his face. "And proof of residence? A utility bill, recent bank statement?"

Matt swallowed. "My Delaware incorporator assured me that active contracts and invoices would show legitimacy. These show both business activity and an address." Matt tried not to blink, every nerve expecting her to call his bluff. A bead of sweat slid down his temple.

She let the silence stretch, then said, "It may be sufficient. Our compliance department will decide."

Matt nodded, but inside his chest tightened.

Andrea tapped her pen on the desk. "One more thing. This department monitors accounts for suspicious activity. Sudden large deposits of anything over $10,000 or unusual transfers may trigger reviews, which can sometimes lead to audits. Do you understand?"

Matt forced another smile. "Absolutely. I plan for it to hold modest savings or consulting income only. Nothing irregular."

"Perfect," she responded with an air of skepticism. "The account will be USD-based. However, it will remain pending until compliance signs off and your first wire deposit clears. Only then will it be active."

Matt nodded in approval.

She photocopied his passport and his driver's license and took possession of the other documents. Then she smiled, though it felt professional, not warm.

"You'll receive confirmation by post at the address on file. If compliance requires more, they will contact you. Do not transact until you are notified." She handed him a slip of paper with routing information and a temporary account number. Her grip lingered just long enough to feel like a reminder.

Matt forced a polite smile, thanked her, and walked out into the blazing sun, the weight of her steady gaze still clinging to his back. The heat hit him like a curtain. He kept walking, heart pounding, until the knot in his chest loosened.

It hadn't been easy. Every step of that meeting had felt like a test, as if one wrong word would send him tumbling. Now, holding the bank papers in his hand, the weight of what he'd done settled in. *It was real.*

He had created something separate, secret, and potentially dangerous. The thought of moving money, of testing whether his quiet code could bridge worlds, pressed at the edge of his mind.

And yet, as he flagged a cab back to the resort, a strange calm overtook him. He told himself it was relief. But deep down, he knew it was anticipation—the first step toward something larger he had not dared to name.

THAT NIGHT, they dined under the stars again. Bernice was radiant after her spa day, skin glowing, hair pinned back. They shared a bottle of Sauvignon Blanc and fresh lobster over rice.

"So," Matt said after the first course. "I did something today."

She looked at him, amused. "Do I want to know?"

"I opened that savings account we talked about."

Her brow lifted. "You didn't waste any time, did you?"

He nodded. "Just a little one. Dollar-based. For us. For the future."

She stared at him.

"I know I said to go for it, but I just want to make sure we aren't setting aside too much for *somedays* or *maybes*. We have the mortgage payment coming up soon, and your student loans are still being paid off."

"Don't worry," he reassured her. "I'm not talking about wiring all of our savings. I'm talking about a hundred here, a hundred there. Just something to build a nest egg. A dream account."

She believed him, yet something in his tone unsettled her—it carried weight, intention. She felt a flicker of unease, as if he was already halfway down a road she hadn't agreed to travel.

Back in the room, the night still warm and the waves whispering beyond the patio, they undressed slowly. There was no rush. The island, the wine, the feeling of shared conspiracy, all of it lingered in their touches. And for a little while, it really felt as though *someday* had already begun.

CHAPTER 18
CONTROL TEST

The first thing anyone noticed when Matt walked into the office on Monday morning at exactly 8:00 a.m. was the tan. Not the faint flush of a weekend outdoors, but a deep, golden bronze. Caribbean, unmistakable.

"Well, look who found the sun," Royland called from the far end of the bullpen.

Ray Oh let out a low whistle. "Damn, Goose Man. You look like you've been living on a beach."

Matt laughed. "Something like that."

He dropped his backpack by his desk, sat down, and powered up his terminal. His chair sagged in familiar discomfort, and the screens around the office flickered with the same stale dashboards. A printer in the corner clicked and whirred, spitting out paper with a dry rasp. Yet none of it touched him. He still carried salt in his hair, the ghost of sunscreen on his skin, and the weight of the ocean in his chest.

By 10 a.m., Derek strolled in late, coffee in hand, tie crooked as always. The smell of burnt espresso clung to him as he leaned against Matt's cubicle wall.

"All right, George Hamilton," he said. "Let me catch you up on what you missed."

Matt swiveled in his chair, half-expecting a crisis.

Derek shrugged. "I have nothing. Absolutely nothing. Same crap, different week. We had a brief outage on Thursday; someone ran a bad script in production. Accounting screamed, then it blew over. Oh, and Randy wants a new aging report by Friday. That's it."

Matt nodded. "Got it."

And just like that, he was back. Yet beneath the surface calm, his mind hummed. He couldn't stop replaying the sense of being invisible in a system too vast to notice him, and the quiet thrill of shaping it from within. He told himself it was about fairness, about getting a piece equal to what he gave, but part of him already savored the risk itself.

The next morning, he arrived early.

At 7:15, the office sat in shadow, with only the exit signs glowing red. He liked it that way—the emptiness steadied him. He might have been the first person in the building, so it felt like his.

He logged into Goose and scanned the overnight batch. The faint click of keys echoed in the cavernous quiet. Nothing unusual. By 7:42, he was at the vendor master screen.

He typed carefully:

Vendor Name: Square Consulting LLC

Type: External Vendor: Audit Support

EIN: 94-6217783

Status: Active

Payment Terms: Net 10

Description: Audit reporting: advisory and reconciliation automation.

He checked everything twice. Then clicked *save*. The faint electronic beep of confirmation seemed to hang in the air.

Next, he opened the reporting engine. Five standard exports fed the finance team's reconciliations. He altered each one slightly, inserting a hidden exclusion filter on any vendor tagged Audit Support—a quiet rule buried among valid logic. No one would notice unless they knew where to dig.

The result: Square Consulting LLC disappeared. On paper, it didn't exist.

By 9 a.m., colleagues filed in. The squeak of chair wheels, the hiss of the coffeemaker, and the murmur of morning greetings filled the bullpen. Matt greeted them casually, posturing at some dull task. He waited.

All day, he watched audit queues, security logs, and system dashboards. The cooling fans whirred steadily. No errors. There were no flags and zero alerts. Nothing to see. Each blank screen whispered permission. With every passing hour, the idea that he could outwit the system—take from it unseen—grew from fantasy to inevitability. Yet he knew that certainty came with a price: every keystroke left a trace, every altered report a potential trap. If an auditor stumbled upon the filter, or if the compliance team from their payment bank flagged an unusual pattern, his career could implode overnight. The thought shadowed the silence, making his pulse quicken even as the systems stayed quiet.

Wednesday came—still nothing.

Thursday. Nothing. The silence itself confirmed the deception.

That night at home, Matt sat on the sofa, laptop balanced on his knees, the glow of the screen washing his face. The TV muttered a crime drama in the background, and tinny theme music, but his attention was elsewhere.

Bernice walked in with two mugs of tea, the steam carrying the earthy smell of chamomile, and handed him one. She curled beside him, legs tucked under.

"You've been quiet all week," she said.

Matt looked up. "Just settling back in."

She studied him. "It's more than that. You've got that look.

The one you get when you're building something in your head."

He forced a grin. "You make it sound like I'm plotting a revolution."

"Are you?"

"Not unless accounting reports count as subversive."

She smiled faintly, still unconvinced. "I don't know what it is, but your mind's somewhere else. I can feel it."

He took her hand, her skin warm against his. "I promise it's nothing bad. Just a few things I want to get in motion."

"Like the savings account?"

"Exactly like that. Just ... figuring out how to fund it." At least that part was true.

She leaned against him, letting it go for now. But the pause in her body told him she hadn't stopped thinking. Inside, her mind wandered. She wanted to believe him, to take comfort in his hand and the steadiness of his voice. But she had lived with Matt long enough to know the signs: the half-smile that hid an idea already in motion, the restless energy when his mind was chasing something bigger than he admitted. A part of her was thrilled at his ambition, yet another part feared what it might cost them.

By Friday, Matt let himself exhale. Square Consulting LLC sat quietly in the vendor database, hidden from every normal report. A shadow, a placeholder, a possibility. He doubted even his own Goose teammates could find it.

He hadn't touched the bank account. Not yet. The skimming program still lay dormant in the software stack, waiting. But with no sign of detection, he moved to the next phase.

Across town, Bernice was wrapping up her week, her pen hovering over numbers she couldn't quite add up. The scratch of pencils and the low murmur of office chatter pressed around her, but her focus slipped. She told herself it was work fatigue, but beneath the columns and sums, her mind replayed Matt's distracted look and evasive answers. She debated whether to bring it up that evening, to press him until he finally told her what was going on. But she feared what she might hear, or that confronting him could make the distance between them wider. A faint unease tugged at her, as if he were building something just out of sight. Something potentially unsavory.

What if his "savings account" wasn't as simple as he made it sound? She wanted to trust him, but something in his voice made her wonder if she was already being left outside of a plan he hadn't confessed to. And with that thought came a shiver: if he really was hiding something serious, the fallout could touch both of them; lost jobs, reputations destroyed, even legal trouble. The stakes felt too high for the vagueness she was being asked to accept.

That morning, Matt began coding a new routine, one that would slip unnoticed into the nightly batch cycle. The tap of his fingers on the keys sounded louder than usual, the rhythm of his typing mixing with the faint drone of office machines. He built it in two parts: first, a sweep checking the balance of the dummy account he had created earlier. If it held anything—five dollars, fifty, five hundred—it would trigger a payment instruction. Second, it would generate a payment advice, routing funds as a vendor disbursement to Square Consulting LLC.

The advice mimicked SBF's formatting, passed through the regular queue, and landed in the daily outbound file bound for the company bank. Because it followed protocol, it wouldn't flag a manual review. It looked like any other payout. He reviewed the code three times, combing through it for anything that might trip an alert. Satisfied, he left it in place, scheduled for Monday night.

Finally, he wrote a script that stripped all references to Square Consulting from the digital statements the bank sent monthly, then recompiled the numbers to ensure they added up—a neat job buried deep in the logic.

By 2 p.m., the job had compiled cleanly and passed internal checks. As he sat there, he felt the mix of motives that had driven him this far pressing on his chest. Initially, it was just out of boredom. Now it was more about proving, at least to himself, that he was smarter than everyone else, and moreover, he would eventually be protecting the company. To Matt, Skimming did not feel like theft; in his mind, it wasn't, as he had no intention of actually ever spending the money.

Yet buried under those justifications was the thrill of control, of bending the machine to his will and knowing no one could see it. And hovering over all of it was the risk. If he slipped even once, the system would not forgive him. The bank could freeze the transfers, compliance officers could uncover the anomaly, and auditors could expose the fraud. At best, he would lose his job, his reputation, and Bernice's trust. At worst, he could face indictment, prison, and the permanent ruin of the life he had built. The thought made his pulse quicken, a mix of fear and exhilaration.

The following weekend, Bernice continued to carry her unease with her. Even as they shared quiet meals and ordinary errands, her thoughts kept drifting back to Matt's slippery answers. She noticed the way his fingers drummed too quickly on the table, how his gaze lingered on nothing in particular when she asked about his week. Minor changes in his rhythms, small silences where once he would have filled the air with easy chatter.

She rehearsed questions she might ask, then swallowed them down, afraid of confirming the suspicion that something larger was unfolding behind his calm exterior. At moments, she imagined the worst: whispered judgments from family or the wreckage of their plans if Matt got caught in something he shouldn't be. Or worse.

The fear made her stomach knot, even as she forced a disingenuous smile through their weekend routine. Matt felt it too, in quieter ways: a twinge of guilt when Bernice caught his gaze too long, a spike of paranoia when his laptop buzzed with a bank notification, the sudden thought of men in suits at their door. He told himself it was worth it, that no one could trace what he had built. But the shadow of consequences crept in all the same.

And he knew, with a flicker of awe and dread, that the system—SBF's tried and tested system—would never see it coming.

CHAPTER 19
FIRST FLOW

The following weekend had come and gone in a blur. Friday night found Matt and Bernice back in familiar territory—Johnny MacCracken's in Marietta. Its dim amber lights and the comforting scent of aged wood and spilled beer greeted them like an old friend. The air was thick with the murmur of voices, the scrape of chairs, and the clatter of glasses, while a jukebox crooned faintly and trivia questions were shouted across the bar.

They squeezed into the last available booth with two of their friends, ordered a round of Guinness and the Friday special—fish and chips—and let themselves sink into the rhythm of conversation, laughter, and greasy comfort. Bernice laughed along, yet a small part of her kept drifting back to Matt. She watched him in profile under the amber lights, noting how often his eyes slid away from the group. He laughed at the right moments, but she sensed a distance she couldn't name, a silence tucked inside the noise.

By Saturday morning, they were walking shoulder to shoulder through the farmers' market in the Marietta Square. Bernice lingered at the flower stalls, holding bunches of sunflowers and rosemary, their scents bright and earthy. Matt drifted toward the coffee roaster's stand, where the air was thick with roasted beans, baked cinnamon, and early fall produce. He bought a bag of dark-roast and a loaf of crusty bread, the paper bag warm in his hands. They returned home with a tote full of vegetables and the kind of contented silence that comes from unspoken mutual ease.

Sunday was slower still. They slept late. Matt stayed in his pajamas until mid-afternoon, flipping channels without ever settling on anything, the drone of commercials filling the quiet. Bernice curled beside him with wedding catalogs spread across her lap, circling options and occasionally pointing something out. She tried to picture the two of them on their wedding day; the details she imagined were meant to anchor them, to bring them closer. Yet every time she looked up from the glossy pages, Matt's vacant stare pulled her back into unease.

Matt, though physically present, was only half there. His answers lagged, and his smile was thin. She noticed a heaviness in her chest again but said nothing. When she rose to make tea, she caught his eyes darting toward the muted television's reflection in the darkened window, as if he feared someone might watch from outside. The small flicker of paranoia unsettled her more than his silence.

Monday morning came sharp and gray. As light filtered through the blinds, it felt like a warning. The office parking lot glistened from a slight drizzle. Matt pulled in at 7:55, sipping from a large, toasted-almond coffee he'd picked up at Dunkin' on the way. The sweet, nutty scent filled the cubicle area by the time he dropped into his chair and logged in.

After dwelling on it all weekend, he had made the decision to skim only one in twenty transactions, rather than one in ten. But the logic would remain intact, making it harder to detect and less noisy in the data—a slower bleed.

He waited until the network was quiet—no job runs, no login congestion—and pushed the code just after 8:10. It compiled. Seamlessly. No flags. He sat back for a moment, heart thudding, and watched the time-stamped deployment scroll across the lower log window.

Then, in an instant, the new code was live. Matt could feel the adrenaline rush through his veins.

By 10:00, the team had filtered in. Royland arrived first, complaining about traffic on I-75. Ray trailed behind with a gas-station cup and a chocolate bar in his jacket pocket. Derek made his usual entrance 30 minutes later, carrying a half-eaten bagel and an open soda, with crumbs falling to the floor.

The banter resumed as if nothing had changed.

"Matt," Derek called out from two desks over, "is that tan still holding up or did the Georgia humidity bleach it out yet?"

Matt smiled. "Haven't peeled yet, if that's what you're asking."

The rest of the day was a carousel of routine: code reviews, idle chat about football, and a meeting with accounting to clarify a minor technical change on a vendor aging report. Once, a passing comment about "odd report filters" drifted from the accounting side of the floor, making Matt's chest tighten until he realized they were talking about an unrelated vendor issue.

The Goose system purred along. No one questioned anything. Still, twice that morning, Matt noticed Rajive lingering by the server logs longer than usual, his brow furrowed as if puzzling over a line he couldn't place. The moment passed, but it left Matt's stomach tight.

That day, every routine task felt like camouflage, a thin veil over the knowledge of what he had unleashed, and beneath that tension, a complex web of motives stirred. He continued to convince himself it was about showing both how smart he was and how he could save the company from itself. Every now and then, he wondered what he would do with the money if he did actually steal it. Then he came to his senses and reasoned that he would not touch the money; this was just a game.

Yet his thoughts always swung back to his financial position, the weight of student debt, and looming mortgage payments. Could his "game" be his technical lottery win? Sometimes he framed it as a protection for Bernice and the life they wanted to build. Other times, he admitted it was the rush —the power of bending the machine to his will, unseen. He was walking a fine line. But deep in his soul, he knew he was not a criminal.

He couldn't stop imagining scenarios—Derek glancing over and catching a line of altered code, Richard stepping into his cube at the wrong moment, or an auditor raising a quiet flag that would snowball into an investigation. The consequences trailed him like a shadow: job loss, headlines, prison, and the look on Bernice's face if she discovered the truth.

He walked the office floor three times that day, and again on Tuesday and Wednesday, under the pretense of grabbing coffee or checking in with Rajive. His ears strained to catch the tone of side conversations, the cadence of hallway chatter, any sign of technical investigation or buried suspicion. But the office sounded as it always did: keyboards tapping, printers churning, phones ringing—all the mundane urgency of a typical office. The normalcy gnawed at him. Silence, he realized, could be as dangerous as noise.

By Thursday afternoon, he had to remind himself to breathe. Even the harmless sound of a system alert chiming at a nearby desk made his pulse spike, though it was only a low-disk warning for someone else. He found himself watching Derek's monitors when Derek wasn't around, just in case.

That night at home, Bernice caught him staring into the living room, unblinking. "You're doing it again," she said from the kitchen, the smell of sauteed onions drifting into the room.

"Doing what?"

"Time traveling. Mentally. Like you're not even here."

He shook his head and laughed it off. "Just work stuff. Month-end is coming up."

She nodded but didn't smile. She knew his attention was elsewhere, and the hollow feeling it left sat heavy in her chest. In her quieter moments, she wondered what he could possibly be hiding that drew him so far away. *A secret at work? Another life?* The possibilities made her pulse quicken, each one more unsettling than the last.

That Friday afternoon, four days before month-end, the office was unusually quiet. The sort of quiet that made every keyboard stroke sound accusatory. By 4:45, the Goose bullpen had mostly cleared out. Royland had left early for a dentist appointment, Ray was long gone, and Derek had waved his usual sarcastic goodbye an hour earlier.

Matt stayed behind. The silence pressed on his ears. He thought he heard footsteps in the corridor and froze, half-expecting someone to appear, before realizing it was only the building's HVAC groaning to life. He sat at his desk, double-clicked an internal tool, and ran a query against the dummy account. A figure appeared at the bottom of the screen:

$615.70.

He stared at the number. It wasn't life-changing. It wouldn't buy him more than a round-trip flight and a hotel room. But it was real. It was proof. Proof that the system had delivered what didn't belong to him, and no one, not a soul, had noticed. His throat went dry. He was still staring when a voice made him jump.

"What's keeping you here this late, Matt?"

He spun around in his chair. Richard Eastman stood at the edge of the cubicle, coffee cup in hand, jacket slung over one shoulder. His expression was light, friendly, normal. But Matt's pulse surged instantly. The edges of his vision wavered for a split second.

"You know it's Friday, right? I'm surprised you're not rushing home to your lovely girlfriend," Richard added with a grin.

Matt swallowed hard. He felt lightheaded, as if gravity had momentarily abandoned its job.

"Just trying to clear my pipeline," he said, forcing a slight chuckle. "Minor report change. Figured I'd get it done while it's quiet."

Richard raised an eyebrow but didn't push. "All right, well, don't let this place suck your weekend away. See you Monday."

Matt nodded, waited until Richard's footsteps faded down the hall, and then slowly turned back to his screen.

$615.70.

It was still there.

He sat back in his chair and exhaled slowly, palms slick with sweat, the whir of the cooling fan loud in his ears. Behind him, a printer coughed to life on auto-schedule, the sudden noise making him jolt. For an instant, he was certain someone else would appear, asking why he was still at his desk.

Saturday night, they drove up to Bernice's parents' house for dinner. The suburban neighborhood looked as though it had been lifted out of a glossy magazine. Two-story brick homes with manicured lawns, kids playing on scooters, and the ever-present scent of barbecue drifting in from someone's back deck.

While Matt and Frank sat in the living room sipping bourbon and watching a Georgia Bulldog college game, Bernice and her mother, Doreen, took over the dining table with a notepad and a pile of RSVP cards. Bernice glanced toward the living room more often than she admitted, straining to hear Matt's tone. To her ears, he sounded light, practiced even, as though keeping up a role. The thought unsettled her, and she forced herself back to the neat lines of the RSVP list. The smell of roast chicken wafted from the oven, filling the house with warmth.

"We're inviting your three teammates and Dennis from work, correct?" Bernice called into the living room.

"Yeah," Matt replied without turning his head. "And if there's space, I'd like to add Rajive and Richard."

"That should be fine," Doreen said. "So that makes it 258 if everyone brings a partner."

Frank raised an eyebrow at Matt with mock horror. "How much is that costing me?"

Matt grinned. "Less than your daughter's smile is worth."

Frank groaned. "You've been practicing that line, haven't you?"

IT WAS the last day of the month.

Matt spent most of the day at his desk, acting like his usual self. He answered emails, fixed a bug in a reconciliation module, and sat through a compliance lunch-and-learn with half the department, pretending to care.

At 6:15 p.m., the office was emptying. Derek gave him a mock salute and said, "Don't work too late. Month-end is always cursed."

Matt nodded, waited 15 minutes, then pulled up the automation dashboard.

The end-of-month batch process would kick off at 8:00 p.m.

His routine was scheduled to run at 8:43. First, it would scan the dummy account, where the skimmed funds had been quietly accumulating. Then, if a non-zero balance existed, it would generate a vendor payment instruction to Square Consulting LLC. That file, like every other vendor payment instruction, would get swept into the outbound payments file directed to the bank. From there, the bank would forward it via SWIFT to the numbered account at the Commonwealth Trust

Bank of Antigua. No extra approvals. No human eyes. Just protocol.

Matt left the office at 7:10, heart drumming against his ribs. He could not sit still during the wait.

Walking through the front door at home, he could smell garlic and onion. Bernice was cooking barefoot, still in her work pants and a loose cotton shirt. He kissed her neck and tried to focus on the rhythm of home: plates clinking, the whir of the ceiling fan, their old Spotify playlist rolling in the background. But every five minutes, he checked the time.

At 8:45, while Bernice was plating the pasta, he excused himself to their bedroom. He opened his laptop and accessed the Goose system through his secure link to verify that the end-of-month batch had completed. Then, using a secure modem line he'd discreetly configured for international dial-up, he connected to the offshore bank's limited-access administrative interface. The connection was slow, painfully slow, but it was enough. Just text-based screens and simple inputs—no graphics, no browser. Primitive, but effective. Still, the connection sputtered twice, nearly timing out. Each hiccup made him imagine an IT admin somewhere noticing the odd traffic and flagging it for review.

One new transaction.

$742.40, Incoming Wire Transfer, SBF

He stared at it for a full minute. For a heartbeat, he imagined the doorknob rattling, Bernice stepping inside to find him hunched over the glow of his laptop. The thought made his throat tighten—how would he explain an offshore bank screen to the woman planning their wedding in the next room? Discovery here would be worse than Richard catching him at work; it would shatter her trust in an instant.

This was the point where his mind started drifting towards what maybe. Could he really steal this money? By now, he had convinced himself that the risk to the business was real. He has proven it.

As he sat there, he considered two options. Stop now and tell Derek and the rest of the team what he had done and why. He could easily close down the Caribbean account and transfer all the money back. Or carry on and potentially take the money.

His hand trembled slightly as he exited the browser and closed the laptop. He stared into the mirror for a second, forcing the expression off his face.

When he returned to the kitchen, Bernice handed him a plate. "Everything okay?"

"Yeah," he said, sitting. "Just thinking about how fast this year's gone by."

She looked at him, then nodded, though her eyes lingered. Inside, a voice whispered doubts she tried to ignore. Still, the distance in his eyes unsettled her.

If it wasn't work stress, what else could it be?

That he might hide something serious lodged itself deeper, leaving her both afraid to ask and more afraid not to. At the table, she watched him chew in silence and felt the dissonance as sharply as a blade: two lives running side by side, hers built on trust, his shadowed by something unspoken. Matt felt it too, catching her gaze fleetingly. He sensed her questions hovering unsaid, but the weight of his choices locked him in silence. He told himself he was protecting her, shielding her from a truth that could break them both; yet, a part of him knew it was also self-preservation, a refusal to risk the only anchor he had.

Outside, the world spun on. But for Matt, every sound in the neighborhood seemed sharper—the slam of a car door outside, the bark of a neighbor's dog, the buzz of the cordless phone on the counter. Each one made him tense, as though discovery lurked just beyond the walls. The fragility of his secret felt one stray glance or misplaced keystroke away from collapse. Bernice thought she saw him flinch when her laptop dinged, and she caught him glancing toward the front window as headlights passed. Small, ordinary moments hinted that his nerves were stretched thin, and she wondered if the truth would eventually spill out through one of those cracks.

Or was she just imagining it all?

The truth was that Matt Hall, sitting at his dinner table, had just moved a few hundred dollars to an untraceable offshore account—without a single soul knowing.

CHAPTER 20
BUILDING PRESSURE

September arrived quietly, with cooler mornings and earlier sunsets. For most people, it meant college football games, pumpkin stands, and back-to-school traffic. For Matt Hall, it meant months of bleeding the system, and no one had noticed.

Every Friday morning, before the first email landed in his inbox, he ran a query against the dummy account inside Goose. The numbers ticked up steadily: $742.40 after the first transfer, then $983.10, then $1,134.95. Not huge amounts, but clean, quiet, and invisible.

At each month-end, the funds slipped offshore just as he'd designed. A SWIFT confirmation. Then, 10 days later, a paper statement from Commonwealth Trust Bank of Antigua. Cream-colored envelope, faint watermark, no logo. He always got to it first, sliding it into the back of his closet, folded inside a leather-bound notebook beneath old tax returns.

He never touched the money. He kept telling himself he never would.

It's just a test—a favor, he repeated. *Proof of concept.*

He wasn't buying watches or booking villas. He wasn't a thief, just a man who had proved the system could be beaten.

Still, the guilt hung on him like a fever. It buzzed in his head when he brushed his teeth. It tightened his chest while Bernice talked about floral arrangements or resort options in Antigua. Some nights, he lay awake, thinking of wiping it all, deleting the vendor, scrubbing the logs. No one would ever know. Or maybe they would. Maybe Derek already suspected.

He cut the thought short, rolling onto his side, heart hammering. But he didn't stop.

They closed on the townhouse on Cole Street in the second week of September, the first real milestone of Matt's adult life. Friends and family packed the narrow red-brick building with chatter, laughter, and the clatter of boxes. The air smelled of fresh paint, new carpet, coffee, and sugar glaze from the tray Bernice's mother carried in. Even Derek showed up, muttering congratulations before slipping out again. The house itself stood proudly with its white trim and creaky iron railing, which Matt secretly liked. Nestled on a quiet block shaded by oaks, it felt less like a purchase and more like a flag planted, proof they were building something permanent.

The move was exhausting but oddly satisfying. Bernice labeled boxes with precision. Matt hauled furniture with Frank and one of Bernice's cousins. The new place had more of every-thing—light, space, privacy. That first night, surrounded by unopened boxes, they ate Thai food cross-legged on the floor and toasted with paper cups of cheap fizzy wine.

"I still can't believe it's ours," Bernice said.

"Neither can I."

Matt smiled, but the weight on his shoulders never left. Even as they unpacked, his thoughts strayed south, to that account in Antigua, swelling quietly in the background. What if someone on the Goose team stumbled across it tomorrow? What if something errored out and it forced one of them to investigate? He forced the thoughts away, shaking his head as if it would vanish if he moved fast enough. But the thoughts of his skimming project consumed him. One minute it was a thrill, the next he was filled with dread. In a moment of clarity, he asked himself if it was worth it. The truth was, he still didn't know.

Bernice glowed that month. Some of it was the new house. Some of it was the wedding, nine months away. Mostly, it was the job offer.

Coca-Cola.

She'd interviewed a few weeks earlier, nudged by a university friend in finance. The role was a junior contract and budgeting analyst, but it came with better pay, fantastic benefits, and the cachet of that red-and-white logo.

"They said I'll be working with the international bottling groups," she told him one night, as Matt unpacked bags of apples and onions.

"That's amazing," he said. "You're going to take it, right?"

She hesitated, twisting the edge of the offer packet. "It's a commute. And I feel bad leaving Atlanta United. But … it's Coke. Even my dad couldn't stop grinning. He said, 'You'll be the breadwinner now.'"

Matt kissed the top of her head, catching the faint scent of her shampoo. "You'd be crazy not to. I've always planned to be a kept man."

She laughed. "That's what I needed to hear."

The next day, she accepted.

For Bernice, it felt like forward motion: her career was rising, their home was settled, and the wedding was ahead. In quiet moments, though, she noticed Matt's distance. The way his shoulders tensed at the mail. The silences that stretched too long. She told herself it was stress. Sometimes she feared it was something else.

At work, Matt felt suffocated. The software bugs were trivial. New features amounted to "lipstick patches." Meetings dragged. The only spark came from checking his code, verifying the exclusion filters, watching the sweeps go unnoticed.

The dummy account now averaged $400 to $550 a week.

No one had noticed. *Not once.*

He listened to Derek complain about compile times and Royland argue with the infrastructure team about printers. Matt thought, *I've built a shadow system under your noses, and you still think toner is the problem.*

One morning after a minor freeze in Goose, Derek muttered, "Systems always bleed somewhere. The trick is hiding the mess." He grinned faintly.

Matt laughed, but the words stuck like a splinter. *Did Derek know? Or was it just a joke? Or worse, was he testing him?* Matt's throat went dry. He spun back to his screen and clicked aimlessly, as though busyness might drown the thought.

The thrill and the disgust mixed within him. It was like standing on a rooftop ledge, half wanting to step back, half wanting to lean forward and ... he stopped that train of thought, pulse racing, hands slick.

Home offered a different rhythm. On Wednesday nights, they walked through the neighborhood. Bernice found a wooded path that led to a bakery she called "their place." Saturday mornings smelled of croissants, coffee, and sugar dust. Sometimes Matt read the paper while she planned centerpieces. Sometimes they sat in silence. Those silences grew heavier. Once, as a siren passed, Matt snapped his head up, eyes wide, before forcing a laugh.

Wedding talk carried a constant tally of costs, venue deposits, catering, and flowers. Bernice mentioned that flowers alone might cost several thousand dollars. Matt nodded. "We'll figure it out." His smile was thin. "Somehow."

Nearly seven grand sat offshore while he clipped grocery coupons. *If only I could ... no. Not yet. Not ever.*

Bernice seemed happy. That was his saving grace. She didn't know.

The only flare of tension came one Saturday when she reached the mail first. Sorting bills and catalogs, her hand stopped on the cream-colored envelope with the Antigua postmark. The paper felt heavier, deliberate.

"What's this?" she asked.

Matt's stomach dropped. "That? Oh, it's just a statement for the savings account we set up on the trip. Remember?"

She paused, trying to pull the memory.

"And they're mailing us statements. Really? Can they just email them?"

"It's the Caribbean," he said too quickly. "Not exactly the most modern banking system."

She tilted her head, lips parting as if she had another question, then let it go.

She handed it over, but her eyes lingered on his for a moment before she turned away. Later upstairs, she remembered how fast he'd pocketed it. The unease lingered.

In the bathroom, Matt unfolded it. $6,812.90—Account Balance.

He stared until his vision blurred. What if Bernice had opened it? What if, He shoved the thought aside, crumpling the paper slightly in his grip?

That night, he stood in the kitchen, the fridge humming, the faint smell of curry from dinner still in the air. A car rolled past, headlights sweeping across the blinds, and his pulse spiked as if it might stop outside.

He spread the statement on the counter. Nearly $7,000. Money that no one authorized. Money no one missed. He had beaten the system. Everything he had identified as a concern, he had proven. And now, he didn't know what to do with it. Burn it? Transfer more? Shut it down? Each option flashed and disappeared before he could finish the thought.

He folded the paper and tucked it out of sight in his pocket.

When Bernice came downstairs and wrapped her arms around his waist, he kissed her forehead. "I was just thinking," he whispered. "Maybe we should go to the bakery tomorrow."

She nodded against his chest. "Mm, sure."

His heartbeat thudded unevenly beneath her cheek. She thought of the envelope, the flicker in his eyes. "Matt, are you —" She stopped herself. "Never mind."

Later, lying awake, she replayed it all and knew that whatever he was hiding was already shaping the life they were building.

In the window's dark reflection, Matt saw himself, pale, tense. He may have been losing weight, but he was clutching a secret no one could ever know. For a moment, he imagined Bernice uncovering it, and the thought chilled him more than the September air seeping through the frame.

CHAPTER 21
NEW POSITION

By mid-October, the rhythm of Matt's days had settled into something dangerously close to complacency. The townhouse on Cole Street was finally starting to feel like home, and the hidden offshore account was now holding just over $9,000. He checked it once a week, always after Bernice had gone to bed, always with a tight, guilty knot in his stomach. He knew nothing would change until the end of the month, but still, he checked. The skimming system ran silently, invisibly, like a submarine beneath calm waters. And yet, every time he logged in, a jolt of panic reminded him that this was real money, accumulating under his name in a place he should never have touched.

At work, though, it was becoming clear to others, especially Derek, that Matt's attention was drifting. He still showed up on time, still delivered clean code, but the energy was missing. Derek mentioned it in passing to Rajive, his tone deliberately casual. Rajive, after mulling it over, decided it might be time to re-engage Matt with something new.

A week later, Matt got a calendar invite for a private meeting with Rajive.

"Nothing serious," Rajive had said when they crossed paths in the hallway. "Just want to pick your brain."

They met for nearly an hour in Rajive's cramped corner office, the blinds half-drawn, sunlight pooling across a messy table strewn with product roadmaps and compliance memos. Outside, traffic hummed, and the occasional honk pierced through the slatted blinds. They talked about the firm, the direction of the tech division, and Matt's future.

"You've been an asset from the start," Rajive said, pausing to adjust his glasses, "but it feels like you're coasting. That's not a criticism. It's just … I think you're ready for more."

Matt nodded, careful not to overplay his excitement. "Me too. I've felt that. I'm ready."

It was genuine. He meant it. But beneath the words was a small, nagging voice reminding him that the higher he climbed, the greater the fall would be if anyone ever uncovered the account.

The following week, another meeting appeared on his schedule, this one with Rajive and Richard Eastman. Matt arrived a few minutes early and found both men already seated, sipping coffee that filled the office with its bitter, nutty aroma, and talking in low tones. The moment felt heavier, more formal.

Richard smiled as Matt entered. "Have a seat."

What followed was a long discussion about the firm's next phase, market competition, tightening margins, and the urgent push toward an IPO. Richard noted a slight dip in overall revenue in one of the regional reports; nothing catastrophic, but enough to raise eyebrows at the board level.

Matt felt his chest tighten. The amounts were small in the dummy account, but they were real. Real enough to add up over time. He shifted in his seat, the squeak of the leather under him loud in his ears, adjusting his posture. "Right, yeah," he said quickly, trying to focus as Richard pressed on.

"With the IPO process well underway, every percentage point now carries weight," Richard explained. "Every inefficiency is under the microscope, and no deviation will go unexamined for long."

Matt nodded along, his expression neutral, but inside, his mind was roaring. It was the first time he truly grasped that his side project, once a private proof-of-concept, might one day be the loose thread that unravels everything.

Richard leaned back. "Transaction intelligence is something we're falling behind in. We need smarter pricing, faster reactions to risk. We want to develop a new transaction pricing engine from scratch. And we want you to lead it."

Matt blinked. "Lead it?"

Richard nodded. "We're promoting you to senior developer. You'll have two junior developers reporting to you. First crack at management. Congratulations."

Matt was stunned. And thrilled. And terrified. Recognition should have felt like validation, but instead, it made the secret account feel heavier, as though the new title shone a brighter light on every shadow.

"That also comes with a raise," Rajive added. "Twenty thousand."

Matt managed a smile, though his voice wavered. "That's ... wow. Thank you." His mind raced. He still thought he was underpaid for the caliber of his work, but $20,000 meant pride, security, and a chance to breathe easier about the wedding. It also meant more visibility, more eyes on him, and higher expectations he might not meet if the secret ever surfaced. A voice in his head whispered that it was now too late to come clean and tell the team about his "experiment." But another voice, darker and sharper, reminded him that if he actually took the money, it could help elevate their life.

That night, Matt burst through the front door of the townhouse and found Bernice in the kitchen, pulling lasagna out of the oven. The air was heavy with the scent of tomatoes and baked cheese.

"I've got news," he said, breathless.

"Good news?" Bernice asked, a grin tugging at her face.

He swept her up in his arms and kissed her again. "They promoted me. Senior Developer. Heading up a brand-new project."

Her face lit up. "Matt! That's amazing! What kind of project?"

He gave her a quick summary: automated prices, smarter decision-making, building something new. She peppered him with questions, and he loved every single one.

"And a raise." He grinned. "Twenty thousand."

She let out a low whistle. "Well then. We really are moving up."

They opened a bottle of wine, its sharp cork-and-berry scent filling the kitchen. Music hummed faintly from a radio on the counter as they danced around the room, clumsy yet joyous, and ended the night tangled together beneath fresh bed sheets. Bernice lay awake longer than Matt, her head on his chest, listening to his heartbeat. She told herself it was excitement that made it race, but a small corner of her wondered if it was something else.

By the end of the week, the transition had begun. They relocated Matt from the Goose team area to a smaller, glass-walled room on the opposite side of the floor. His new team—two junior software developers named Luis and Charlene—was eager but green. His first act as manager was to whiteboard a roadmap. The squeak of marker against glass echoed too loudly in the small room, the smell of Camdens clinging to the air.

Richard was clear: the pricing engine was urgent. New entrants in the MCA space were already eating into SBF's market share.

Matt dove in with real purpose, sketching out the architecture, assigning research tasks, blocking out dependencies. The tempo of his days changed instantly. He was no longer reacting; he was building.

But on Monday morning, when he logged into his new machine, the first thing he noticed was a permissions error.

Access denied: Goose Application.

He tried again—same result.

"Come on ..." he muttered. His hand hovered over the mouse, pulse quickening, blood pressure rising. For the first time, he realized he was cut off from the one thing that bound him to the fraud.

They'd revoked his access. Of course, from SBF's point of view, he no longer needed to get into Goose.

He froze. The faint hum of the office HVAC pressed into his ears. There was now no way he could check the dummy account or make any changes. He planted that worry in the back of his mind and returned to reviewing the morning's emails.

Later that day, Derek wandered past his new office, poked his head in, and smirked. "It's strange not seeing you buried in Goose anymore. You used to live in there."

Matt forced a laugh. "Guess they've moved me up in the world." The comment was tossed off lightly, but it lodged like a splinter.

At home, wedding plans had shifted into high gear. Doreen had finally completed the guest list, and RSVP cards had trickled in. Envelopes lay scattered across the kitchen table.

"We got a *yes* from all of your family," Bernice told him one evening while sorting envelopes. "And Dennis too."

Matt looked up from his laptop. "Did Richard respond?"

"Not yet. But I think he'll come."

Bernice had grown into her new job at Coca-Cola with surprising ease. She talked about bottling schedules, freight costs, and SAP workflows over dinner. She'd even brought home a Coke-branded fleece jacket and insisted Matt try it on.

"It's a little big," he said, tugging at the sleeve.

"That's the point. *Cozy*," she replied, wrapping her arms around him. Her smile was bright, but she noticed the way his arms felt rigid beneath the fabric, as though his body were present while his mind lingered elsewhere.

Their relationship had settled into something loving and genuine, still filled with spark but now grounded in routine and shared direction. Even though they had both increased their salaries, financial worries bubbled up in quiet moments, with Bernice fretting over wedding catering costs and her mother hinting at the cost of flowers. Matt smiled and told her not to worry, but she sensed a strain in the way he said it, his voice a beat too quick, his smile a shade too tight.

In the evenings, they would sit on the small back patio of their townhouse, drinking iced tea as they listened to cicadas and watched dusk settle over the rows of identical rooftops. The smell of cut grass sometimes drifted from a house facing them. Bernice would read aloud from wedding magazines, her voice light and hopeful, while Matt leaned back in a deck chair, pretending to focus but quietly slipping into thought.

She noticed when his gaze drifted too long, when his answers came too late. She never pressed, but each moment etched itself deeper into her growing unease.

Matt's parents had called the night after his promotion. "We're proud of you, son," his father had said, his voice crackling faintly over the line. "This sounds like a proper step up."

Matt smiled. "Thanks, Dad."

Bernice, listening from across the room, had smiled too. But later, alone in the bedroom, she saw Matt slip something from his bag and slide it quietly into the closet. She didn't ask, but the image lingered in her mind.

Later that night, Matt opened the latest Antigua bank statement, crisp with newness.

$10,482.35.

His access to Goose was gone. The system was running autonomously now. Each Friday, another few hundred dollars slipped through the cracks and at the end of every month, surfaced offshore.

He could no longer check the logs. No longer fiddle with the filters.

It suddenly dawned on him that he couldn't shut it off. He had wanted to. He told himself that constantly. But when he finally decided to shut the whole thing down, they had revoked his access to Goose. The very tools he'd used to orchestrate the skimming were no longer available to him. Ironically, *it was the system's own security* that now prevented him from ending the fraud. And so the machine ran on, detached from its maker, while Matt lived knowing that even if he wanted to do the right thing, he no longer had the means to do so.

He folded the statement and placed it in the envelope with the others, hidden deep in the closet. Bernice, brushing her teeth in the bathroom, caught the faint sound of the drawer closing and wondered again what it was he always kept tucked away.

Then he turned out the light and went to bed.

Fall was in full swing. The leaves outside their townhouse had all fallen, now crunching underfoot. The wedding seemed to be so far away, yet just around the corner.

Matt Hall had stepped into the spotlight. Promotion. Managing a team, and with it a bright future. And somewhere far beneath it all, and now outside of his control, his illicit code still hummed like a ghost in the system, waiting to be found.

CHAPTER 22
APPROACHING WALL

By mid-November, the pricing engine project was humming. Matt had convinced Richard to allow him to develop the application using a new rapid application development tool called RapDev, which he had recently discovered. It was a risk, but if it performed as Matt believed, it would allow his small team to build the application quickly, a risk he felt was worth taking. Still, he carried a nagging concern, as Rajive had warned him; he was putting his career on the line if it didn't work out.

Matt and his team quickly built an early prototype, impressing Dennis and the technology management team during a Friday demo. The prototype earned them a rare, understated nod from the CTO that lingered in Matt's mind far longer than it should have. His new team—Charlene, quick with ideas but sometimes scatterbrained, and Luis, quiet but methodical—had gelled surprisingly well. The pace was fast, the deadlines close, and Matt felt productive for the first time in weeks. *Almost.*

Beneath the polished sprint boards and the drone of daily standups, the skimming system he'd built continued to siphon funds like a clockwork parasite.

Each Friday, more dollars vanished into the void that was the dummy account. Matt no longer knew the details. He couldn't access Goose. He couldn't stop it. It was now a machine, self-sustaining and autonomous. Each month, the envelope would arrive from Antigua with the printed bank statement inside, stamped and folded with bureaucratic neatness. The stiff paper smelled faintly of sea air, as though the island itself clung to it. He hid them behind a row of tax forms in the upstairs closet, their musty paper scent masking the truth.

As of mid-December, the account held $12,785.90.

He sometimes caught himself calculating the interest it might earn or drifting into half-dreams about what the money could do for them: a down payment, a new car, even the Antigua bungalow they once joked about. Then the shame would pull him back—sharp, sudden.

Stop thinking. Don't even go there. It's poison. And if they ever found out? Fired. Arrested. Wedding canceled. Life shredded.

One gray Thursday afternoon, Rajive poked his head into Matt's office. "Quick heads-up," he said. "I've just been told that Ed Cushin and Dennis have completed their work for the lead in the IPO. They've engaged Morgan Stanley as the book runner. They're sending in a full team in January to complete their due diligence. We'll be getting a full audit. Systems, books, risk models, the works."

Matt froze. "January?" His voice cracked slightly, and he coughed to cover it.

"First full week," Rajive said, already halfway down the hall. "Don't worry, it's mostly finance and ops. You're not the target."

Not the target. The words rang hollow.

Audit. January. Too soon—too close.

He stared at his monitor, heart thudding in his ears. The fluorescent lights above buzzed like a swarm of bees. He'd expected scrutiny eventually, but this soon? If the auditors pulled one wrong thread, even a minor anomaly, his name, his access history, his fingerprints could surface. *Prison*, he thought of the word and shoved it down, but it clung like tar.

THAT YEAR, Christmas became a formality for Matt, an obligation that barely registered against the drumbeat of fear in his chest. They flew to New York on December 21st, landing at LaGuardia just as a dirty snowstorm rolled in from the Atlantic. The plane rattled as it descended, the stale cabin air thick with the scent of recycled coffee and perfume. Bernice had insisted on visiting his parents this year, despite his evasiveness. She knew something was wrong. He hadn't been sleeping, hadn't been eating properly, and she had noticed that he had lost weight. He'd withdrawn so far inward that even his jokes had stopped landing. She told herself it was stress, but at night she lay awake listening to his restless breathing and wondered if there was something worse, something he hadn't shared.

Matt's parents lived in a modest two-story walk-up on a quiet block in Bay Ridge, Brooklyn. His mother, ever the holiday traditionalist, had covered the railings and windows with lights and garlands. The smell of nutmeg and roast ham hit them before they reached the kitchen. His father, a former MTA train driver with hands like baseball mitts, shook Matt's hand a little too long.

Later that evening, while Bernice helped his mom wrap the last of the presents, scissors snipping, tape sticking to her fingertips, Matt stood on the tiny back deck with his father, both men nursing beers and watching snow collect on the rusted grill. The cold bit through his sweater; the metal railing stung with frost.

"You all right, son?" his dad asked. Not as a challenge. As a father.

Matt hesitated. "Work's just been … intense."

Intense—weak word. Pathetic.

He hated the way it sounded. And if he said more? Confessed? His father would never look at him the same way again. His father nodded but didn't speak.

Inside, Bernice heard them through the glass, the muffled cadence of voices and the faint clink of bottles. She said nothing but tucked the thought away. She was growing used to observing him from a distance, cataloging every hesitation, every sigh. It hurt that he could open up even a little to his father but not to her.

Christmas Day was subdued. Bernice wore a deep burgundy wrap dress with gold earrings, elegant and understated. Her laughter rang out like bells against the muted clatter of cutlery and the soft carols playing on the stereo. Clare, his sister, arrived with her two boys in tow. They erupted through the front door like small hurricanes, scattering wrapping paper and demanding cookies. Clare gave Matt a long hug.

"You look pale … and thinner," she whispered.

"Work," he replied, not meeting her eyes.

How long could he keep saying that? He asked himself. *Keep blaming work? And if she pushed, what then? What could he tell her? That he'd built a crime into the backbone of his career.*

Bernice noticed that too. She always did. She was torn between confronting him and protecting him, but chose a stinging silence.

After dinner, as the family settled into the living room, Clare found Matt alone in the kitchen, staring out at the dark yard. Snow had crusted over the trash cans. A lone suburban raccoon shuffled past the fence line, filling the silence.

"Is Bernice okay?" she asked.

He turned slowly. "Why wouldn't she be?" Too defensive. Idiot.

"Because you're not. And she knows it. You think she doesn't notice?"

He said nothing. What could he say? *Yes, she notices that he's drowning, and that if anyone at work dug too deep, he could face a perp walk instead of a wedding aisle?*

She leaned in. "Whatever this is, you either fix it or come clean. You don't get to live in the middle. It eats people alive."

Bernice, coming into the doorway with a tray of steaming mugs, caught just enough of Clare's voice to know they were talking about her. The scent of cocoa curled up from the cups as she forced a smile, but her chest tightened. She wondered how long she could go on loving a man who seemed to slip further away from her every day.

Later that night, in the guest room, Bernice curled beside him and traced her finger along his shoulder blade.

"They're worried about you," she whispered.

"I know."

"So am I ... the wedding, Matt. We need to make some choices soon. My mom says the florist's deposit is due. And the catering costs are higher than we budgeted."

He swallowed hard, shame cutting deeper. "I'll handle it," he blurted.

Handle it how? With what? He didn't know. At that point, he had no idea. He knew only that if the wrong auditor found the wrong file, he'd be handling it from a jail cell.

She held his gaze for a moment, then rested her head on his chest. His heartbeat thudded unevenly beneath her ear. He pulled her close but said nothing. She felt the distance in his silence and thought: *if he couldn't share the truth with her now, what would their marriage look like?*

After Christmas, they traveled back to Atlanta.

Their townhouse looked lifeless in the cold post-holiday light. The flight back had been silent. Matt sat by the window and pretended to sleep. Bernice watched him and thought of all the times she had done the same, pretended not to see, not to know.

On New Year's Eve, they stayed home. Bernice made linguine and opened a bottle of champagne. The kitchen filled with the scent of garlic and simmering tomatoes. When midnight came, she kissed him tenderly.

"This is our year," she said. "A fresh start."

She meant it, willed it, prayed for it. But when he nodded, she felt the hollowness in it. And in that hollow space, a question formed: *fresh start from what?*

THE JANUARY AUDIT was days away.

By the second week of January, the diligence team had arrived. Morgan Stanley didn't send accountants; they sent an assassin, a senior director, and a group of kids—young surgical consultants in dark suits and monochrome ties. All just out of college and eager to impress. Their shoes squeaked on the linoleum as they fanned out through the building like colonists: interviewing, inspecting, cataloging.

Matt kept to his corner, head down.

On Wednesday, word circulated that the auditors had flagged a dormant test account in Goose, one that had cleared no transactions in over six months but still showed a positive balance. Derek was approached for his thoughts, and, as expected, he just shrugged it off.

"Probably a leftover from some old QA tests," he told Richard with a breezy ease that felt too practiced. "We had loads of those. I'm sure if they looked, there'd be a few more. We use these to test our work."

Still, due diligence required asking around. Derek pinged the Goose team and then wandered over to Matt's desk later that afternoon.

"Hey, you remember setting up a dummy account for payment testing back in the spring? Something labeled SB4140X-Demo?"

Matt's spine prickled. "Hmm. Rings a bell. We had a bunch of those, didn't we? Just sandbox stuff. I don't think we ever used that one in prod." *Keep it casual. Don't over-explain. Don't let him see the sweat.*

Derek scratched his chin. "That's what I figured. Told Richard it was probably just an orphaned test record. Funny how these always seem to turn up." His tone was light, but his eyes held the faint glimmer of someone fishing.

"Sounds right," Matt said. "No idea if it's still active."

Derek nodded, already moving on. "All good. Just needed to close the loop."

The exchange was brief, unremarkable—precisely what Matt had hoped for. But that night, alone with the latest Antigua bank statement in hand, his nerves frayed further. If Derek ever pulled the wrong report, if Richard ever asked for a full audit trail—done. He would be ruined.

That night, he sat in the townhouse study with the door closed. Bernice was in the bedroom, on the phone with her mother, going over wedding logistics and muttering about ballooning costs. She felt both exasperated and alone in the planning, but what unsettled her most was the muffled sound of Matt moving papers behind the closed door. The shuffle of envelopes, the faint scrape of a chair; the kind of noises that carried secrets—secrets that gnawed at her.

Matt pulled out the latest bank statement from Antigua.

$14,139.75.

It was too much. Too exposed. He had to shut it off.

But he couldn't.

He no longer had access to the Goose platform. Not as an admin. Not even as a read-only user. He'd considered asking Derek to reinstate him under the guise of helping with historical reports, but quickly ruled it out. Derek was too sharp. Too close to the system. Any such request would raise questions Matt couldn't answer.

He toyed with the idea of finding a technical backdoor. Writing a simple ping utility to test endpoints. Looking for an exploit.

But that was fantasy.

So, the code ran. And the account grew. And every night, he died a little more inside.

Stop. Don't think about it.

But he did. Every night. And if the auditors linked it back—handcuffs. Trials. His parents watching him on the news. Bernice walking away for good.

On Friday, Charlene brought in donuts for the team. The sugary smell filled the little office.

"You look rough," she said, handing him a coffee.

"Didn't sleep well," Matt replied.

In fact, he hadn't slept at all. Just stared at the ceiling until dawn, imagining FBI agents at his door.

She tilted her head. "You sure you're okay? The auditors asked me some nonsense about access logs this morning."

He gave a small laugh that fell flat. "Yeah. Just tired."

Just tired ... I am always tired. Liar. And if she kept pressing, would she stumble upon it too?

When the day ended, he stayed behind, pretending to finish a requirements doc. He waited until the floor was quiet—the hum of the vents the only sound—then opened a terminal and tried to access Goose. He tried numerous development accounts, but none of the passwords he tried worked.

He felt watched.

Not by people, but by the system itself. And in that moment, he thought he heard the faintest echo of his own code whispering back at him.

Stop imagining things. It's code, not a ghost.

But it felt alive. And if it betrayed him—if a single anomaly surfaced—the auditors wouldn't hesitate. They'd tear him apart.

THAT WEEKEND, Bernice cornered him.

"Talk to me. If not about work, then about us."

"What do you mean?"

"I mean, you're barely here. Physically, sure. But your head's somewhere else. We're getting married in a few months, and I feel like I'm losing you."

He looked at her then, really looked. Her eyes glistened, but she didn't cry.

As she stood there, Bernice thought of how many times she'd swallowed her questions, how often she'd told herself to wait for him to open up. And now she couldn't wait anymore.

"If you can't tell me what's wrong now, when will you? After the wedding? After it's too late?"

He opened his mouth, closed it, opened it again. Nothing came.

Say something. Anything.

But his throat locked. And all he could picture was her, testifying one day, spilling her guts to some jury—people she would never actually know but would be in charge of deciding her fate.

Instead, he pulled her close and rested her head against his chest. She held him like something breakable, but inside, she felt something break in herself, too.

Outside, the wind rattled the bare trees, their branches scratching the night like bars on a cage. And inside, Matt Hall clung to a life he no longer fully controlled.

CHAPTER 23

CURVE OF THE SPIRAL

T he IPO due diligence audit was finally over. Morgan Stanley's team had packed up two days before the end of January and flown back to New York, leaving behind a wake of stress, broken printers, and drained staff.

Matt had watched them go with a mix of disbelief and awe. They hadn't found it. Not the heartbeat script, not the skimming account, not even the shadow log file that briefly stored encrypted totals before purging itself each night. Moreover, their team had not identified the payments to Antigua.

Richard had handled it perfectly. When the senior Morgan Stanley director, a graying, sharp-eyed man named Hollis, asked about the dormant Goose account labeled SB9148X-Dummy, Richard brushed it off.

"Just a legacy QA sandbox," he'd said. "We use those for internal load simulations. It's closed."

Hollis had raised an eyebrow.

But then he'd turned back to the parade of rookie investment auditors shadowing him, fresh graduates from Dartmouth and NYU, earnest and eager but green as spring grass, and moved on. *Box ticked.* Two weeks later, Dennis and Ed Cushin, the firm's sole owner, were presented with the full findings. "SBF will be an A-grade investment. No major risk factors identified."

The words made their way onto a glossy Morgan Stanley slide deck and into Dennis' mouth at the next all-hands meeting.

"We've cleared the due diligence phase," Dennis announced with a grin. "Morgan Stanley's rating is one of the strongest they've issued this year. We've been greenlit for our target-filing window."

The room erupted in applause.

Matt clapped too, just enough to avoid suspicion. But his mind wasn't in the room. It was back in the codebase of Goose, in the quiet, recursive routine he'd written more than a year ago. That loop still ran. That account still grew. And the auditors—one experienced man and five glorified interns—had missed it all. He learned something that day. Never fear the system. Fear the people. Most of them aren't even looking.

If life were simple, he would've been happy. He had a beautiful fiancée, a new townhouse in a great neighborhood, and a senior developer title with a fast-track to management. He should've been floating.

Instead, he was unraveling.

Each week, when Bernice went to her spin class or ran errands, Matt would log in to the account on his laptop. Sometimes twice. Sometimes three times in a single evening, refreshing the screen even when he knew deposits only posted at month's end. Just to see. Just to feel the jolt of numbers growing. On the last Friday of every month, the envelope from Antigua would arrive—clean, clinical, and damning. He'd wait until she was asleep, then pull it from the stack of mail and slip into the study to read it in silence.

By late February, the account held $54,210.90.

It was growing faster than ever.

SBF's merchant portfolio was expanding. New clients. New volume. More skims.

It terrified him. And yet, in darker moments, he caught himself thinking about what the money could buy: a bigger house, a honeymoon beyond their budget, an emergency cushion to put Bernice's mind at ease. The temptation shamed him, but it never entirely left.

Everyone noticed that Matt was growing increasingly distant.

At work, Charlene mentioned he seemed distracted, though she said it with a smile and a jelly donut in hand. Luis said nothing but had started double-checking Matt's documentation, as if expecting him to miss something.

At home, it was impossible to hide. Bernice had been patient, brilliantly so, but even she was reaching her limit. She asked fewer questions and offered more silence, which Matt knew was worse. Silence meant she was deciding how much of herself to protect. She had begun cataloging his moods like weather patterns, storm fronts rolling in, sunny spells that never lasted. It wore on her. She wondered sometimes if marrying him meant inheriting a life of half-truths.

Clare had called twice after a Sunday brunch and said only, "You don't sound like yourself."

During a weekend visit to Marietta, Matt's mother pulled Bernice aside.

"He's holding something in," she said. "I've seen that look before. It's the same look his father had the year he retired."

Bernice smiled politely, but inside, her stomach twisted. She hated that even his mother could see it.

It was now just months before their wedding; they had decided to have dinner at Il Sogno, a cozy Italian place Bernice had loved since their early days in Atlanta. The restaurant smelled of garlic and charred bread, the low rumble of conversation punctuated by clinking glasses. She wore a slim, cream-colored blouse and pearl earrings, with soft makeup that framed her blue eyes. Matt barely touched his food.

She waited until the check came. The candle flickered between them, throwing shadows across his face.

"Are you having second thoughts?" She finally said it. She feared the answer, even though she'd wanted to ask for months.

Matt looked up, stunned. "About what?" His voice cracked slightly.

She gave him a tight smile. "The wedding. *Us*."

"No," he said quickly, but it came out defensively, too sharp.

"Then what is it? Because I'm walking into a marriage with someone I barely recognize anymore. I'm not stupid, Matt. I know something's wrong. And I know that even after our recent pay raises, the bills are mounting. My mom told me today the caterer wants another deposit."

He stared at the candle, its tiny flame bending in the draft. Behind her, a server poured Chianti at another table. He opened his mouth, then closed it again.

"I want to tell you," he said finally, his voice hoarse. "It's not what you think, Bernice. It's not about us. I just need some space to sort out my work stuff. I love you more than anything; you are my life, my everything."

Bernice studied him—the way his eyes darted instead of meeting hers, the sheen of sweat at his temple. He said he loved her, but it felt as if he were pleading with himself as much as with her.

She reached across the table and took his hand. Her palm was warm and steady, but her thoughts churned.

"I love you," she said. "But this feels like watching you drown and not being allowed to throw you a rope."

"I'm not drowning," he said quietly. The lie scraped his throat raw. His mind screamed: *You're drowning, and you'll take her with you.*

She squeezed his hand. "Then swim, Matt."

THAT NIGHT, he lay awake, watching the ceiling fan spin. He almost told her then, words pressing against his throat, but he swallowed them back down.

Tell her what? That I built a parasite into Goose, and now I can't kill it? She'd leave. She should leave.

He couldn't say it.

The account wouldn't stop. And he couldn't kill it. He'd tried imagining a thousand scenarios: calling Derek, faking a need for data access, writing a kill script from the outside, but none of them worked. He was locked out. The mechanism he built was out of his hands. And worse, in his darkest paranoia, he wondered: *If Derek looked too closely, would he notice the seams? Would he see what Matt had done?*

On Friday after work, he sat in the study with the envelope from Antigua. The house was quiet except for the tick of the wall clock and Bernice's faint humming upstairs.

He rubbed his eyes and stared at the wall.

He wasn't even angry anymore.

He was exhausted.

And the worst part was, no one had made him skim the money. It was just a challenge to himself; no pressure, no blackmail, no genuine financial desperation. Just a moment of egotistical brilliance that initiated a "test"—now completely out of control.

A FEW WEEKS LATER, they picked up Bernice's wedding dress from the dressmaker. She glowed with joy as she turned in the mirror, lace and satin catching the light. She looked at him through the glass, hoping for a reaction, some reflection of the life they were building. He smiled, and for a second, believed it. She wanted to believe it too, but deep down, she sensed the distance behind the smile.

He would not let this thing destroy her. Or them.

He would find a way to fix it. Somehow.

Even if it meant destroying the career he'd built. Or losing everything else he thought he controlled.

CHAPTER 24
WEDDING BELLS

It was now early July. The wedding arrangements had pulled Matt away from other things, and he found the past few months to be a welcome distraction from constantly worrying about the skimming software and the growing balance.

Getting measured for the suits, ordering the rings, planning —and executing—the bachelor party—wedding prep had been all-consuming, and he loved it. For the first time in many months, he was sleeping well.

On the morning of the wedding, the sun crept across the hardwood floors of the Marietta Inn, casting a warm amber light through the cream linen curtains.

Matt stood at the window of his suite, sipping weak coffee and watching the parking lot slowly fill with guests. Like most grooms, he was nervous after a sleepless night. Yet, as the coffee kicked in, he felt a wave of excitement radiate through his body. The room was quiet except for the occasional knocks and distant voices down the hallway. Outside, the southern summer was steaming. He opened his window and could smell the newly cut grass and white dogwood blossoms floating past like confetti.

After a while, the coffee high diminished. He should've felt joy. Their wedding day. But for some reason, his mind went back to the skim. In no time, his chest was once again in a knot, twisted by guilt, fear, and anticipation. His palms sweated, his hands trembled, and a dull headache had settled at the base of his skull. He rubbed at his temples, but the pressure stayed.

The last time he checked the Antigua account, it held over $76,000. The code still ran. The skimming process still worked. And he still had no way of stopping it.

By noon, he'd already had a few glasses of Glenfiddich. Nerves, guilt, fear—they all tasted the same now. The edge was dulled, but the dread remained.

Down the hall, the bridal suite buzzed with activity. Clare was doing her makeup while Bernice sat in a robe, hair halfway pinned, champagne flute untouched. She smiled often, but her eyes flicked toward the door every time footsteps passed. Her mother, radiant in a lavender dress and brimming with anxious energy, fluttered around the room like a general on a campaign.

"Where's the florist? I told them noon sharp," she muttered, smoothing nonexistent wrinkles from the table linen. "Clare, are those the shoes or the backup pair? Lord, we're already running behind. And considering the money we spent on this wedding ... it better be perfect."

"Mom," Bernice said gently, "breathe."

Her mother paused, hand on her chest. "I know, baby. I just want everything to be perfect. My only daughter, getting married." She sniffed and dabbed at her eyes with a tissue, then turned briskly back to directing the chaos. "Who's got the rings? Has anyone seen my clutch?"

Clare caught a glimpse of Bernice's reflection. "You good, Bernie?"

Bernice nodded. "I think so."

Clare studied her. "You don't sound sure."

"I am. It's just ... Matt's been so very distant lately."

"Cold feet?"

"No," Bernice said firmly. "Not that. Something else. I think it's work-related, but he's so tight-lipped about it."

Clare didn't press, but her brow furrowed slightly as she glanced toward Bernice's untouched champagne. She set down the mascara wand and knelt beside her soon-to-be sister-in-law.

"Are you sure everything's okay?" she asked softly.

Bernice hesitated, then nodded again, more convincingly this time. "Yeah. Just nerves, I guess."

Clare offered a knowing smile, but her eyes lingered on Bernice a beat longer, as if weighing whether to say more.

Her mother peeked her head back in. "They're ready downstairs. Let's move!"

They held the ceremony on a manicured, bright green lawn under a white gazebo, which was decorated with garlands of spring roses. Friends and family filled the folding chairs on either side of the aisle, faces beaming beneath pastel hats and linen suits. Bernice's mother dabbed at her eyes with a monogrammed handkerchief as the music swelled.

Matt stood at the altar with his best man, Ray, feeling as if he were watching the scene from outside his body. He saw Bernice turn the corner, dress floating like a cloud behind her, eyes locked on him. His heartbeat increased, and overwhelming love flowed freely through his entire body.

For a moment, everything else disappeared: the weight of the account, the dread of discovery, the guilt that had eaten away at him for months. All of it fell away as he watched Bernice move toward him, radiant in white. She looked like a dream stitched from light and grace, and the look in her eyes held such unwavering love that it momentarily lifted the crushing burden on his back. For the first time in many months, he felt joy.

Her father gave her away with trembling hands. When she reached Matt, she whispered, "You look terrified."

"I am," he whispered back. "Terrified of how lucky I am."

She gave him a searching look, as though trying to pierce the distance she still sensed. But she centered herself, remaining composed, and smiled softly as the ceremony began.

Vows were recited. Rings exchanged. Applause rang out. Cameras flashed.

Within 30 minutes, they were married.

They held the reception at a converted barn on the outskirts of town, which had candles, string lights, and a local jazz quartet. It was warm, lively, and full of laughter. Bernice changed into a sleek satin dress for dancing, while Matt remained in his tailored suit, top button undone, tie slightly askew by hour two.

Bernice's mother made the rounds like a diplomat, thanking every guest and fussing endlessly over Bernice. "Drink something, sweetheart. Have you eaten? Those little bites won't carry you through the evening ... you need some real food."

After consuming a significant amount of wine, she commandeered the mic for an impromptu toast, dabbing her eyes again.

"I always knew my daughter would find someone special, but I never dreamed she'd find someone as smart, kind, and decent as Matthew." She raised her glass. "To the Hall family!"

Matt laughed where appropriate, clinked glasses with distant cousins, and even danced with his mother, which was a first. But beneath it all, he felt the weight, a pressure starting to once again build in his temples, a guilt that no champagne could dissolve.

It was after the first toast that Dennis cornered him.

"Matt, come walk with me for a second," he said, bourbon in hand, his words slightly slurred.

They stepped outside into the cool night air, the sound of laughter muffled behind them.

Dennis leaned on the wooden railing and sighed.

"You've done well, kid. Really well. Everyone's noticed. The new system you developed is really helping us gain more market share."

Matt nodded, wary.

Dennis continued, voice dropping. "Look, I'm probably not supposed to say this. But you should know … the IPO may not happen."

Matt's chest seized.

"What?"

"Yeah. Ed's talking to a FinTech company in New Jersey, Summit Funding Partners. They've approached him about an outright buyout. He's considering it. Said it might be a cleaner exit for him. Less paperwork. More money."

Matt tried to keep his tone steady. "That is technically a takeover; what would that mean for the rest of us?"

Dennis snorted. "Probably not much. Maybe retention bonuses for senior folks. But the rank and file? Doubt they'll see anything. You included, I'm afraid."

Matt looked down at his shoes. "Why are you telling me this?"

Dennis shrugged. "Because I like you. And because I'm a little drunk." He chuckled. "Oh, and Richard Eastman resigned last week."

Matt's head snapped up. "What?"

"Yeah. Didn't tell many people," he said. "Felt burned out, I guess. Although I suspect that once he heard the IPO was almost certainly off, he decided he wanted out. He didn't even show up today. Shame, really."

Matt didn't respond; up until that point, he hadn't realized that Richard was not there. His mind flickered, unbidden, to Goose.

If Richard were gone, Derek would have more say. And if Derek ever dug too deep, would he see the seams of what Matt had built? Or worse, would he look the other way, as if he'd always known?

Dennis clapped him on the back. "Forget I said anything. Go enjoy your night, Mr. Newlywed."

He vanished back into the barn.

Matt stood there alone for a long time. The sky above was clear, stars blinking gently down like silent judges. The temperature was starting to fall, a welcome relief from the stifling commotion inside.

Richard was gone. The IPO is likely dead. And the code still ran.

Unstoppable, and—as far as he knew—untraceable.

Inside, Bernice was laughing with Clare, her eyes sparkling under the lights. She caught his gaze and smiled, waving him in.

He forced himself to smile back.

AFTER SPENDING their wedding night in the bridal suite of the St. Regis Atlanta, they boarded the flight to Antigua— their favorite destination. The next morning, they were tired, slightly hungover, and wrapped in that surreal post-wedding glow. Bernice held his hand during takeoff, her head resting on his shoulder. She looked peaceful. Content.

Matt closed his eyes and tried to be present. But his thoughts raced. Richard would be gone when he gets back to the office. He thought about Dennis' warning, and a creeping fear arose that his perfect moment had a hollow foundation.

Somewhere, a system still skimmed thousands of dollars.

And Matt could not stop it.

CHAPTER 25
PRESSURE IN PARADISE

The plane touched down at V.C. Bird International Airport just after 2:15 p.m., the sun casting long shadows across the tarmac as the newlyweds once again stepped into the humid Caribbean embrace. Antigua smelled of salt mixed with jasmine, pulling them instantly back to their first visit. A soft breeze carried the sea air, and though Matt wore only a loose shirt and chinos, sweat gathered at the base of his neck. Bernice, radiant in a cream sundress, floppy hat, and oversized sunglasses, gripped his hand as they walked toward customs. Descending the plane's steps, they looked the part of a Hollywood couple beginning their honeymoon. Bernice felt a swell of joy but couldn't help noticing the way Matt's smile flickered, how his eyes seemed to drift, even in this paradise.

The island's quieter southern coast hosted the Calypso Sands resort, tucked between two crescent beaches lined with palms and hibiscus. Their driver greeted them at the airport with a placard and a grin, pressing cool towels into their hands as they got into the car. The 30-minute drive wound past quaint pastel houses, children chasing soccer balls, and fruit stands stacked with mangoes. Bernice pressed her forehead against the glass, pointing things out and laughing easily. Matt forced himself to respond, though his gaze lingered on a pickup game of cricket. She leaned her head on his shoulder, choosing not to press him. This was their honeymoon; she wanted the island to mend what silence had frayed.

Their room was even better than before: a standalone cabana with vaulted ceilings that caught the late sunlight, a private plunge pool that shimmered turquoise, and wide curtains framing an endless stretch of ocean. Inside, the cool air smelled of cedar and tangy citrus, laced with the faint sweetness of fresh-cut flowers. Outside, waves whispered steadily against the sand, mingling with birdsong and the faint rustle of palm fronds. The floor tiles held a trace of sea salt, and the entire space felt alive with color: ivory walls, teal cushions, the golden glow of the sinking sun spilling across the bed.

"Can you believe this?" Bernice asked, spinning barefoot across the tile. She thought of all the years ahead, hoping this place might loosen whatever weighed him down.

Matt set their bags down, pulling Bernice into an impulsive kiss, the kind that came from being young and restless. She laughed against his mouth, tugging him toward the bed.

"Feels like we're trespassing in someone else's fantasy," he murmured between kisses, already undoing the buttons on her dress as sunlight spilled across the sheets.

That night, showered and sun-drowsy, they ate at the beachside restaurant, sand still clinging to their ankles. The menu, printed fresh on heavy cream stock, listed lobster bisque, grilled mahi-mahi with papaya salsa, and snapper wrapped in banana leaves. Matt hesitated at the prices, but Bernice squeezed his hand, reminding him it was their honeymoon. They ordered cocktails; she had a rum punch, and he had a dark and stormy. They shared the bisque to start. Torches hissed and flickered against the surf, the air rich with the scent of charred fish, citrus, and the sweetness of burning coconut husks.

Midway through dinner, Bernice laced her fingers through his. "So ... can we afford that little yellow cottage on the hill?" She said it lightly, but her eyes studied him. She pictured the gingerbread-shaped house often, a life simple and uncluttered.

He almost choked on his wine. "What?"

She smiled. "The one we saw last time. The one I loved."

He forced a laugh. "It probably sold already .... Besides, Bernie, we've got a mortgage now."

"True," she said, catching the flicker of tension across his face as the torches hissed and a waft of charred coconut husk drifted between them. She swirled her wine, watching the deep red catch the firelight. "Still ... wouldn't it be something? A little house like that, shutters painted turquoise, sea air in every room." She tilted her head, teasing. "What about the dream account we opened last time we were here? Any money there?"

For a moment, Matt froze. She hadn't mentioned it for months. "No, just the seed money," he blurted.

Bernice let it go with a smile, but inside, she felt the distance again; mention of that account had jarred him. He grinned, but the laughter never reached his eyes.

The week passed in a haze of sun and salt—lazy mornings, snorkeling, afternoons napping in cabanas. Bernice wore sundresses and straw hats. Matt rotated swim trunks, sandals, and his UConn baseball hat. They spent evenings at candlelit tables with steel drums in the background. Bernice felt blissful, though each time his gaze traveled a bit too long out to sea, worry pinched her chest. She tried not to let it ruin things, but part of him always seemed to be elsewhere.

For Matt, dread never left. He hadn't touched the Antigua funds, hadn't planned to. Yet each dawn, while Bernice still slept, he checked the balance on his laptop with the room's complimentary, albeit slow, dial-up connection. Inside, he knew the numbers would not change mid-month, deposits only posted at month's end, but the act had become a compulsion, an addiction even, a ritual he could not break. After multiple dropped connections and painfully slow page loads, he saw it. His pulse quickened, guilt and relief colliding at the sight: $83,500. And growing.

What chilled him was how basic it really was. He'd written a small script inside Goose that skimmed a few cents from roughly one in twenty transactions. He shuffled those tiny amounts into a fake clearing account and, at midnight, labeled them as routine fees before sending them offshore at month-end. No one ever checked the logs that closely, line by line, so it stayed invisible.

To make sure, he'd built in a cleanup command that wiped temporary records every few days and intercepted incoming digital bank statements, erasing transactions tied to the Antigua account, then rebuilding them with false totals before accounting ever saw them.

It was simple, almost too simple—and that simplicity scared him now. Moreover, the code was buried so deep inside Goose that no one would ever find it. Unless, of course, your name was Derek.

He erased the browsing history on his laptop each time he checked the account, telling himself he wasn't "using it" if he never withdrew a cent. But the script was alive. The money multiplied.

On a beach walk, Bernice looped her arm through his. "You've been quiet."

"Just soaking it in."

"Promise me we'll always come back here. No matter what." She studied him. "And maybe put that laptop away sometimes."

He watched the horizon, the sun a molten coin slipping under the sea. His shoulders were tense as he crossed his arms tightly, as if bracing against a storm. His jaw was set, and he shifted his weight from one foot to the other before finally answering. "Promise."

Bernice smiled, but she noted his tension. She tucked away the moment, sensing his promise might not mean the same to him as it did to her.

On their last evening, he stood ankle-deep in the surf, the sky streaked purple and gold. Bernice called from their cabana. He didn't move; he was totally lost in his thoughts. Even on his honeymoon, the constant nag of what he had done was consuming him. She noticed.

They boarded their return flight that Sunday; Matt was strangely relieved, while Bernice sensed something vital had been left unspoken.

***

A FEW MONTHS HAD PASSED, and summer storms drummed outside as they cleared dinner plates. They had settled into the normal newlywed rhythm of work, hanging with friends, and lots of sex. For a while, Bernice worried less about Matt.

That night, as the storms continued to rumble, Bernice poured a glass of sparkling water, her hand brushing her stomach. She had rehearsed this moment for hours.

"A delicate glass of white wine for my lady?" Matt announced with a smile.

She shook her head. "Actually ... no."

His brow furrowed, eyes widening, his head tilting back slightly in open surprise.

She smiled nervously, her eyes shining with anticipation and fear, her lips trembling as she searched his face for a reaction.

"I'm pregnant—" The words tumbled out, half joy, half fear, her expression a fragile mix of hope and uncertainty.

Matt froze. The silence stretched.

"I know we weren't trying," she added quickly. "It just ... happened."

He blinked, then laughed, deep and genuine. "Oh, my God. We're going to be parents?"

Bernice nodded, tears shining. "I found out this morning."

He pulled her close, kissing her face again and again, laughing through the kisses with a rush of giddy excitement. "I can't believe this. I feel so lucky ... but terrified ... but so damn happy."

For a split second, the thought flared in his mind: the skimmed money could keep them safe, could pay for doctors, diapers, a future. His chest swelled with excitement, but he forced that thought away, crushing it down, still telling himself he would never touch that money.

They held each other, swaying as rain tapped against the glass. Bernice rested her hand on her belly, letting herself believe in his laughter.

NEWS SPREAD QUICKLY. Bernice's mother wept with joy. Matt's mother sent a blanket she'd knitted by hand. Friends toasted them at Hemingway's, the clink of beer bottles marking Baby Hall's due date in mid-1998.

After the initial burst of joy, Matt should have felt elated. Instead, just as the decline of a sugar rush, the weight of the Goose skim pressed down harder.

At work, Richard Eastman's absence lingered like a shadow across the entire division. Richard had set the tone—casual, collaborative, more mentor than manager. With him gone, the atmosphere shifted overnight, growing colder, more formal, and far less forgiving.

By early autumn, his replacement arrived: William Brooks,

known in Atlanta tech circles as Billy B—a mid-fifties, tall, broad-shouldered man with slicked-back silver hair and a faint southern drawl. A former Regions Bank executive, he favored tailored navy suits and polished shoes that clicked sharply on the tile. His manner left no room for excuses; where Richard had been loose and approachable, Billy was controlled, deliberate, and precise.

Within weeks of his arrival, he redrew reporting lines, imposed committees, and demanded formal documentation for every system change. He prowled unannounced, eyes sharp, a fixer known for exposing weaknesses others overlooked. In meetings, his clipped tone and habit of jotting names in a small leather notebook made developers uneasy. Nothing slipped by him.

Soon, he brought in Julian Petrov as head of internal data security. Petrov had the air of a man used to secrets, short, stocky, shoulders squared like a bulldog, and a stare that lingered just a beat too long. Born and raised in Russia, he spoke with a heavy accent, his English precise but clipped, with rolled Rs and a low growl in his tone. He had come from defense contracting, dismantling systems piece by piece until flaws revealed themselves, and he carried that same relentlessness here. He ordered access logs with blunt authority, ran penetration reviews personally, and summoned staff behind closed doors with a quiet menace that left people sweating. His reputation for digging until something cracked preceded him, and whispers spread quickly through the office.

The news chilled Matt—reviews, logs, audits. Any of them could shine a light on his code. Although the software was buried deep, woven into legacy COBOL, he knew that Derek still had access.

What would happen if Derek helped with an audit of the Goose system?

Billy B. wasn't the kind to let things slide. And Petrov, with his Russian growl and bulldog stare, wasn't the kind to miss ghosts hiding in the code. His very presence made developers sit straighter, feeling as if he were judging every keystroke.

One crisp morning, everyone received an email from Dennis: an all-hands staff meeting was scheduled for that day. No details, only brief instructions for everyone to attend.

Nearly a hundred staff jammed shoulder to shoulder into the ground-floor atrium, the air thick with chatter, coughs, and the scrape of shoes echoing on tile. The noise swelled—gossip about bonuses, IPO dreams, rumors of takeovers—before settling into a charged hush as leadership stepped forward.

The company owner, Ed Cushin, joined Dennis, but it was Dennis who took the mic.

"For a while now, we've been exploring strategic options in parallel to managing through the proposed IPO," he began. "Recently, Summit Funding Partners, one of our biggest competitors out of New Jersey, approached Ed directly about a buyout. After some consideration, Ed has pursued the Summit offer. With that in mind, they have begun formal due diligence. They're considering gaining Sunbelt outright."

A ripple spread. Matt sat in the back, heart hammering. The news of Bernice's newly revealed pregnancy still rang in his mind—family ahead, risk closing in.

His thoughts raced: *would a buyout mean his job vanished overnight? Worse, would Summit's auditors peel apart Goose line by line, uncovering the script he had buried?*

The idea of losing everything—career, freedom, the chance to be a father without a cloud hanging over him—made his stomach twist.

Questions from the staff flew:

"Will we get stock?"

"What about bonuses?"

"Do we still go public?"

Ed offered vague assurances. Most faces brightened. A buyout meant growth. Validation.

Matt saw only peril: auditors, forensics, outsiders digging.

That night, Bernice slept soundly, hand on her stomach. Matt sat in the dark, his laptop open.

Credentials, redirect, account number.

$92,315.30.

His chest clenched. The skim was speeding up. New clients? More volume? He didn't know. He only knew at this point that he couldn't stop it.

He closed the laptop softly, the room reclaiming its quiet. His heart thudded in the dark. His ghost script kept siphoning cents. It was buried so well that it looked like noise, no patterns, and completely harmless, unless someone dug deep. And if Summit's auditors dug, they would find it.

CHAPTER 26
WALLS CLOSE IN

Two months had passed since the company-wide meeting. The legal component of the sale to Summit had been quickly completed. What remained was the hard work, the physical merger between the two companies.

Antigua felt like a dream now, faded like sand washed away by the tide. Back in Marietta, the Georgian winter was fast approaching. The trees along their street had shed their leaves, and mornings carried a faint bite of frost.

Bernice was just starting to feel pregnant. Mornings brought a soft swell beneath her cotton nightshirt. She had experienced a period of morning sickness—the sour taste, the sharp nausea that lingered in the bathroom—but that at least had passed. She stood differently now, hand resting gently on her stomach even when she wasn't thinking about it. Her appetite had shifted to odd cravings—peaches one night, pickles the next. Her moods also rose and dipped like sudden squalls. Matt loved every moment of it. The baby, still the size of a plum, all the books said, had already become a quiet, constant presence in their home.

At night, Bernice curled into him on the couch, her legs tucked under her, asking aloud what he thought it would be:

boy or girl? She wondered what name they might choose. She fretted over nurseries, crib safety ratings, and how they'd ever find a pediatrician they liked. Sometimes she whispered her fears: their money, Matt's distractions, her abilities as a mother. Then she'd laugh, brushing them off, but her eyes constantly searched for reassurance. Matt noticed the faint crease in her brow when she thought he wasn't looking, the way her hand lingered on her stomach as if already guarding something fragile.

On his end, Matt tried to stay present. He smiled more, laughed more, even cracked the occasional joke. Bernice noticed.

"You've been lighter lately," she said one evening over dinner. He was plating stir-fry, the tang of soy and chili rising in the air, his loaded with extra heat, hers mild and fragrant with ginger.

"Really?"

She nodded, chewing slowly, watching him with curiosity. "You've just seemed … less tense. Happier."

He paused, drying his hands on a dish towel rough from too many washes. "I've been thinking about work."

She raised an eyebrow. "Thinking of leaving?"

He nodded. "I think it might be time. The culture's changing. It's not the place I joined."

She considered his words, twirling her fork in the rice. "Then do it. Find somewhere you'll be excited to go every morning. You deserve that."

He leaned across the table and kissed her gently, grateful for the way she always anchored him. "Thanks, Bernie."

That night, though, when Bernice had drifted to sleep, Matt sat awake longer than usual. Her faith in him felt like both a gift and a weight. He thought about the Antigua account. About whether, if anyone ever knew, this fragile sense of happiness could collapse overnight. Bernice shifted in her sleep, murmuring a half-formed word, her hand sliding protectively across the small curve of her belly. He wondered what she would think if she knew. The thought made his throat tighten.

The next morning, he called Ira Rosenburg. He hadn't spoken to him since joining SBF. He explained that he felt it was time to seek a new opportunity. Ira warned him that the job market was tough, but promised to look into it. After hanging up, Matt felt a wave of relief wash over him, almost dizzying in its suddenness. For a brief moment, he imagined himself walking cleanly away from SBF, from Goose, from the skimming code, from the gnawing paranoia.

At work, SBF had transformed. New rules and fresh eyes had smothered the old culture, which had been loose, improvisational, and almost playful. Before, the Goose team had fixed problems on the fly, fueled by pizza boxes and inside jokes. Now the halls carried an unfamiliar sound: the heavy shuffle of auditors, the clipped tones of managers, the silence of developers too nervous to talk. Even the smell had changed—less coffee and fried chicken, more disinfectant and printer toner.

Summit Funding Partners—once one of SBF's fiercest competitors—had by now completed the legal takeover, and with it came surprises Matt had not expected. He had assumed that in any acquisition, the buyer would sweep away the old systems, move customer and vendor accounts onto their own platforms, and close out the legacy SBF ledgers. He braced himself for exactly that, knowing it would almost certainly expose the ghost process. But two very unexpected things happened.

First, the combined business abandoned the Summit name and kept SBF's brand. Second—and far more critically—they decided to continue running on the SBF operating platforms, Goose included. Even the bank accounts, with their old wire instructions, stayed untouched. The decision left Matt baffled and reeling. Yet, he felt a surge of relief. If Summit had forced migrations and reconciliations, they would have flushed out his little parasite. Instead, it lived on, hidden in plain sight, flowing invisibly and unbroken.

Matt's relief lingered, but the new head of internal data security, Julian Petrov, quickly undercut it. Petrov had built out his team, hiring two analysts with government-grade credentials. The three of them now patrolled the infrastructure like a private militia.

Every week brought a new rule: stricter permissions, mandatory reviews, new logging protocols, encrypted vaults for code pushes. Developers grumbled in hushed tones, watching years of informal privilege get dismantled. The easy camaraderie of the Goose team shrank in the wake of his presence.

Some of Petrov's reputation came from more than his résumé. Rumors swirled that he had once overseen data compliance for a Russian defense contractor, where a single mistake could cost more than a job.

He never confirmed it, but the way he studied people—eyes flat, expression unreadable—suggested a man trained to spot weakness and exploit it. His motivation seemed clear enough: to build an empire of control, one where nothing slipped through without his knowing.

The Goose team, once carefree and loose, felt the shift most.

Ray Oh, the quiet, sharp-eyed South Asian developer who'd been with the company nearly a decade, quit in frustration. He had been the man everyone relied on when Goose buckled under pressure, and his departure sent a shock through the entire technology division.

"I didn't sign up to be policed like a high school kid," he told Matt on his last day. "All these tickets and approval forms —I used to fix things in minutes. Now it takes hours. It's not fun anymore. And the promise of an IPO and its rewards have just been smoke."

Matt had no answer, just a handshake and a sad nod. Ray had been the best man at his wedding; losing him felt like losing family.

Ray's departure rippled outward. The younger developers, who once leaned on him for guidance, now seemed adrift. Conversations that had carried bursts of laughter and confidence were now hushed. Even Derek, usually brash and unflappable, grew quieter, his jokes landing less often. Whiteboards, previously brimming with wild ideas, sat clean and untouched, and the internal message system now sat eerily subdued. It was as if Ray had carried with him the last of their confidence when he walked out the door.

The contrast between the old and new SBF grew sharper daily. Where Richard had tolerated chaos so long as results came fast, Billy B's regime demanded process, paperwork, and order. Developers used to slap code into production in minutes. Now, every change required three approvals and a signed ticket. And Friday afternoons sharing beers in the bullpen—gone. The place that had once felt like a startup now felt like a stuffy bank branch office. And everyone—from coders to accountants —knew it.

Bernice noticed the change too; Matt came home tighter, quieter, stressed. She would rub his shoulders and coax him to talk, but he always gave half-answers, leaving her wondering what he wasn't saying. Still, she stayed patient, believing that her steadiness might one day pull him back.

And hanging over it all was Summit's integration team. Thirty people strong. Golf shirts, slacks, clipboards, and cold northern accents. They flooded the office atrium during their first week, their chatter loud and boisterous. Staff whispered nervously as the outsiders set up camp, gossip flying about what they were looking for.

"They're here to tear us apart."

"No, it's just standard integration."

"Why so many of them then?"

Every passing comment felt like a test.

The Georgia staff grumbled about the clash: how Summit's own MCA processes were sloppy compared to Sunbelt's, and how ironic it was that the buyer seemed less professional than the one being bought.

Bernice caught wind of these complaints through Matt's offhand remarks and pressed him gently, sensing his unease. He brushed her off, claiming it was just a cultural clash. But his eyes gave away more—a flicker of fear.

Matt kept his head down. The skimming code was buried, obscure, deep inside a legacy module. He convinced himself that if Goose remained, finding it would be almost impossible. Still, the paranoia never left him. A laugh across the hall, a Summit auditor's raised brow—any of it could make him sweat through his shirt.

He felt hunted. Not just technically. Spiritually.

Dennis, once the life of the office—high-fiving interns, joking with janitors, filling rooms with cigar smoke and laughter—had all but disappeared. He skipped happy hour and left meetings early. His talk was all about golf communities in Florida, RV catalogs, and grandchildren not yet born.

"That man has already retired," Derek muttered to Matt one afternoon. "He just forgot to stop collecting the paycheck."

But Dennis' withdrawal wasn't only about golf courses and the Florida sun. Matt sensed a man who had played the game too long and finally saw the walls closing in. Dennis had been part of every backroom deal, every risky client that made SBF rich. Now, with Summit's auditors circling, he looked less like a leader and more like someone planning an exit strategy.

"Funny thing is, back in the day, Dennis used to dabble in writing his own 'shortcuts' for Goose," Derek commented, smirking. "Real cowboy stuff. Half the mess we clean up now started with him."

The comment slid off as banter, but it stuck with Matt. Derek never elaborated, and Matt didn't press. Still, the thought that someone else had once buried their own hidden code inside Goose gnawed at him.

SBF no longer felt like SBF. It felt like a company waiting to be swallowed. And yet, perversely, business was booming. At a rare staff meeting, Dennis informed the team that revenue was through the roof. Every week brought new merchant clients. The credit card sweeps were increasing. The risk models, now semi-automated, were outperforming expectations. Money was flying in. Even amid the chaos, the engine was running at full tilt. It was clear why Summit had bought the company.

That night, with Bernice asleep upstairs, her hand once again curled protectively around her stomach, Matt thought of the ballooning sum in Antigua, eating the transaction flow like a fat tick on a healthy dog. He hadn't touched the money. Not a cent. He did not see it as his, but it was real. And it was growing. For a brief second, he thought of cribs and car seats, of Bernice's hand brushing her stomach with that unconscious tenderness. For a while, he let the thought of actually using the money fill his brain. It could potentially change their life. However, if he were caught, that would ruin everything he and Bernice had built. He came to his senses and brushed away actually committing a crime.

CHAPTER 27
CALM BEFORE
THE STORM

L ate December arrived with a brittle calm that threatened to splinter under the smallest pressure. Atlanta mornings gleamed with frost, the lawns silvered, and tree branches etched against a pale sky. Inside the townhouse on Cole Street, warmth clung to every corner. A cinnamon candle burned on the mantel, its sweet spice filling the air. Baby catalogs were sprawled across the coffee table in cheerful disorder. Against one wall leaned a half-assembled crib, pale wood glowing under the lamplight. Weekends had become rituals of anticipation: trips to baby stores, name debates, ultrasound prints tucked into drawers, and moments where Matt's hand found Bernice's belly almost unconsciously.

Bernice radiated energy, not quite showing but already transformed.

She came home from Coca-Cola each day with perfume on her coat and office chatter still on her lips. Mornings, she was buoyant, full of stories and lists for the baby shower. Evenings found her drifting to sleep on the couch before the credits rolled.

Matt would carry her to bed, her weight familiar against him, then lie awake, eyes fixed on the ceiling, his fingers drumming against the mattress while his mind circled endlessly. Sometimes he thought about strollers and pediatricians; more often, his thoughts spiraled toward Antigua, toward numbers on a screen he couldn't ignore. Then his mind drifted back to the office, to Derek's lingering looks and Petrov's new rules. What worried him most was the sense that both the code and the surrounding culture were closing in.

Work continued to shift.

Royland had recently resigned, leaving Derek as its last true keeper. Once sardonic, Derek now carried himself with the quiet confidence of someone who owned the room. He lingered late, green text reflecting in his glasses, fingers tapping with steady patience.

One evening, Matt passed his desk and caught Derek peering at a job schedule report, lips pursed as if he were threading something together. Derek looked up and smiled thinly.

"Funny how some of these old routines run like clockwork," he said.

His tone was light, but his eyes held something heavier. Matt laughed too quickly and walked away, his shoulders tight, pulse racing. He couldn't shake the feeling Derek was cataloging details, collecting breadcrumbs that only he could see.

Julian Petrov's data security group added another layer of pressure. Three people now, moving quietly, pinning laminated rule sheets to corkboards, and speaking in clipped tones under equally unpleasant fluorescent lights. Password resets. Access reviews. Mandatory training. Petrov himself—broad-shouldered, his Russian accent precise as a scalpel—walked the halls like a sentinel.

"We must protect the integrity of the system," he would intone, voice low, eyes flicking over badge swipes and workstation screens. The sound of his heavy shoes on the linoleum made Matt's shoulders knot.

Then came the quarterly project schedule, something Matt had never seen laid out with such formality before. It had Petrov's fingerprints all over it, another of Billy B's new structures, tightening the noose.

Q1 1998: Full System Audit: Project Goose.

Matt's stomach lurched.

Goose.

Right where his code lived, threaded deep into reconciliation jobs and legacy paths. It wasn't visible unless you went looking, but Petrov's team would look. Derek would look. Matt imagined the knock on his office door, the rustle of suits, Bernice's bewildered face as they led him away.

Killing the code would be simple.

A few keystrokes at the right time, a line pulled from the right job. It was all hidden in routines designed to blend in with the noise. Shutting it down could leave audit trails: a gap in the 2:17 a.m. batch, operator commands logged under his ID. Either way, it didn't matter. He no longer had access. The skimming had slipped beyond his control, a ghost he'd unleashed that refused to die.

He told himself it wasn't theft until he touched it, but in his gut, he knew better. If it surfaced, he would lose more than his job; he would go to prison, face headlines, and Bernice would raise their child alone.

Summit's integration team only sharpened the fear. Thirty consultants in brightly colored golf shirts and khaki pants drifted through the office like inspectors at a crime scene, clipboards tucked under their arms, voices clipped and nasal. They poked into processes no one had questioned in years, scribbling notes as if every keystroke might be evidence.

In the cafeteria, staff whispered over coffee:

"They're here to gut us."

"No, they'll just standardize."

"Someone's getting cut; you can feel it."

The noise had an edge of dread. Once, a young auditor asked why jobs ran at night instead of during the day. Matt rubbed his palms against his trousers, gave a plausible answer, but his knee bounced wildly under the table. If they ever turned their eyes on Goose, he knew, the secret would crumble.

Then came the latest company-wide meeting. Dennis looked worn as he adjusted the mic.

"Today marks the next phase: full integration. Effective immediately, all active projects are paused pending review by Summit's integration team."

For many in the room, this was baffling—pausing projects meant halting system upgrades, vendor migrations, and even audits that were already scheduled. Staff whispered: Why would a company stop its own progress? The answer, hinted at in the corporate slides, was that pausing gave the new owners control to examine everything fresh, strip away redundancies, and decide what and who to keep or cut. Murmurs spread hope for some, fear for others, and curiosity for all. Matt barely heard them. His eyes locked on a phrase in the deck: audit pause. They had suspended Goose's audit. Officially, "resource conflicts." Unofficially, it felt like a stay of execution.

Relief hit so hard he ducked into the bathroom, forehead pressed against cold metal, hands gripping his knees, breaths short and shaky.

That weekend, Bernice folded baby blankets upstairs while Matt sat in the garage, the air thick with motor oil and cold cement. He stared at the wall, beer in hand, leg jittering. Could he carry this secret into fatherhood? He imagined Bernice finding out, her face pale, her trust splintering. He pictured holding his child in a prison visiting room. The thought made him shiver.

Later on the couch, Frasier flickered across the TV. Bernice laughed, her belly pressing gently into his side. "You've been better lately," she said, her smile soft. "I think it's the baby. Maybe he's already calming you down."

Matt placed his hand on her belly, nodded, and forced a smile. She told him he'd be a great dad. He kissed her hair, but his eyes stayed fixed on the TV.

Could a man who built his future on stolen money ever be great at anything?

That night, he pressed his hand against Bernice's belly again, searching for the faintest flutter of life. He told himself it would all be okay, that he hadn't ruined it yet.

But Derek's words rang in his head: *ghosts in the code.*

Once a joke. Now seemed like a threat. Matt knew Derek was smart, and with his intimate knowledge of the Goose application, he might be the one to drag his skimming job into the light.

CHAPTER 28
TURNING YEAR

C hristmas 1997 came and went quietly, but not without warmth. This year, Matt and Bernice stayed home in Marietta.

They trimmed the townhouse on Cole Street with garlands and glowing lights, and a modest tree stood in the living room corner with wrapped gifts crowded at its base. The scent of pine needles mingled with cinnamon-scented candles, while the faint crackle of a holiday playlist drifted through the rooms. Bernice, newly greeting her second trimester, moved with a soft, maternal grace that left Matt in constant awe. Her cheeks flushed pink from the winter chill, and her laughter had a ring like silver bells cutting through the cold.

Matt's parents flew in from Brooklyn and stayed with them for a few days. On Christmas Eve, Matt and Bernice, along with both sets of parents, gathered at The Butcher and the Baker, the finest restaurant on Marietta Square.

The town glowed with holiday lights, every tree wrapped in tiny white bulbs, lampposts dressed in wreaths and red bows. The air outside was crisp enough to sting, while the restaurant windows steamed from the warmth inside. Within, the scent of roasted duck and mulled wine mingled with wood-fire smoke.

Glasses clinked, servers weaved between tables, and the room hummed with festive energy.

The evening was close to perfect. There was laughter, gentle teasing, and sentimental toasts. Even Matt, usually guarded, let himself relax into the glow of it all. Matt was relieved when Frank, Bernice's father, paid the bill.

As they readied themselves to leave, Matt caught his reflection in the darkened window; his smile faltered. The light in his eyes seemed dimmer, the guilt tugging at him like an invisible string. Bernice had noticed the way his gaze sometimes drifted; when she laughed with her family, part of her mind always stayed fixed on Matt's distance. Before they stood up, he tightened his hand over hers, as if anchoring himself, but she sensed how much effort it took.

New Year's Eve was quiet—just the two of them. They shared a late dinner fragrant with garlic and rosemary, then curled on the couch for a movie they never finished. By 10, they were in bed. Bernice drifted off quickly, one hand over her belly. Matt stayed awake, restless, the itch to check stronger than ever. He padded downstairs, opened the laptop, and logged into the offshore account.

December 31, 1997: $211,153.70.

The figure burned into him. The balance was getting completely out of control. Summit's takeover had pushed staff harder than ever, driving origination numbers up, polishing the books for integration. Every surge in business meant the parasite swelled. The number glowed like a second life—everything that could save him—and destroy him. He closed the laptop, returned to bed, and whispered, "Happy New Year," into the curve of Bernice's shoulder. She murmured in her sleep, and he lay awake watching shadows shift across the ceiling.

Matt was back at work the day after New Year's. Business was booming, receivables solid, originations brisk. But everything else had ground to a halt. Technology projects? Frozen.

Marketing campaigns? Suspended. They had also paused planned audits. The hallways, once alive with chatter and whiteboard sketches, felt muted, as if the company itself was holding its breath.

What had changed most was the people. That week, around 20 new employees arrived from Summit's head office in New Jersey. They slipped in without fanfare, dressed in sharp suits with precise haircuts, their polished shoes clicking briskly across the tile. Clearly, this was the executive team.

They claimed conference rooms, demanded data reports, spoke in clipped tones behind closed doors. They moved with an air of ownership, not partnership.

The legacy SBF staff were still spooked.

"They're here to gut us."

"No, it's just standard integration."

"A lot of us will be losing our jobs, you can bet on it."

Matt sat in his cube, watching them drift past like surgeons preparing for an operation. He felt no welcome, no hostility—just clinical detachment, as though the entire company was a patient to be opened and examined.

Rumors swirled that Summit might change its mind and merge systems or even flip the business again if returns remained high. For Matt, that sounded like both salvation and doom. If Goose were retired, the code might vanish without a trace, leaving him free. But Derek—or worse, Petrov's team—might notice it before that day came.

For some reason, Derek had grown quieter. He lingered at terminals, eyes narrowing at logs, tilting his head as if listening to something others couldn't hear. Once, Matt caught him staring at the reconciliation queue, lips pressed thin, before Derek looked up with a half-smile that never reached his eyes.

"Funny how clean things look lately," he murmured.

Matt did not understand the comment, but forced a chuckle; the remark stayed with him.

At home, Bernice slowed down. She still worked full days but often came home drained, ankles swollen, back sore.

Matt grew more attentive, cooking, massaging her shoulders, and folding laundry. One evening, as she flipped through a baby-name book with a pencil tucked behind her ear, she paused.

"We should probably think about hospital costs and what the insurance will really cover," she whispered.

The comment was small, but it landed hard. Matt smiled, kissed her hand, and promised they'd manage.

Inside, the knot in his chest tightened. He'd heard from a colleague that delivery bills could top $3,800 even after insurance. The number stuck like a burr. He knew they could scrape by—but he also knew about the shadow balance in Antigua, a forbidden solution he pushed down each time it surfaced. But for the moment, life was quiet. A fragile, deceptive quiet that made him almost believe he'd weathered the storm.

LATER THAT WEEK, Matt's desk phone rang. The number was unfamiliar, but his chest tightened as he picked up. "Matt Hall."

"Hey, kid," came Ira Rosenburg's familiar rasp. "Sorry, I've been MIA. Holidays, you know how it is. But I've got something that just came in."

Matt straightened in his chair. "I'm listening."

"I sent your résumé to Nations Bank. Regional outfit, solid reputation, Charlotte-based. They're expanding their operations group—they need a senior developer with IBM AS/400 experience. You tick a lot of boxes."

Matt blinked. *Nations Bank.* He knew little about them, but the thought of something clean, something free of ghosts, sent a surge of adrenaline through him.

"What did they say?"

"They want to meet you. Interviews are lined up for next week. Could be an excellent fit. No promises, but I've got a good feeling."

Matt leaned back, a smile tugging at his lips for the first time all day. "Thanks, Ira. I needed this."

That evening, he came home with Indian takeout fragrant with cumin and cardamom, and an enormous bunch of red roses. Bernice was on the couch, feet up, baby-name book open.

"Ira called," Matt said, setting down the bag.

Bernice looked up quickly. "Really? Did something come through?"

"Nations Bank. They want to interview me next week."

Her smile bloomed instantly, eyes bright. "Matt, that's amazing."

"I know ... it's such a relief to have forward movement." He sighed. "And of course, these are for you, the mother-to-be— Bernie, I love you so much." He handed her the flowers as he gently kissed her forehead.

She pressed them to her chest, then set them carefully on the table before hugging him tightly. "I love you too," she whispered. "More than you'll ever know."

They sat together, sharing naan and curry from paper cartons, the baby-name book open between them. For the first time in forever, Matt felt the door crack open—an escape, a new beginning. Yet even as he leaned into Bernice's warmth, a shadow thought lingered: could he ever truly walk away, or had he already left too many ghosts behind? He reasoned to himself that he had to man-up and get on with his life. He had not touched the money, had no intention of doing so, and in his mind, he had committed no crime.

I t started with a surprise reassignment.

Since the Summit takeover, Matt had been stuck in limbo—his small team dissolved, his project shelved, his days filled with busywork. Each morning, he came in, performed his minor tasks for eight hours, and then went home, feeling more invisible with every passing week. The quiet had gnawed at him. He missed deadlines, debates, and the pressure of deliveries. Now he was just another shadow in the cubicles.

On a Monday morning that felt like any other, Rajive reached out to him via the internal message system and requested that he come into his office.

"Matt," he said, eyes still on his laptop, "I have some news for you. You're going back to the Goose team."

Matt blinked. "You mean back to developing and supporting Goose?"

Rajive finally looked up. "Donny West asked for you. He's reorganizing the legacy projects. Thinks apart from Derek, you're the one who knows Goose best."

Donny West was one of Summit's imports—mid-forties, wiry, with sharp eyes that missed very little. He dressed with pressed precision, usually in dark suits that fit like uniforms and a silver tie clip always in place. His clipped speech carried the authority of someone used to being obeyed, each word short and deliberate, as though wasted breath was an indulgence he would never allow. When he walked through the office, conversations dropped to whispers. He had the presence of someone who carried both the mandate and the power to end careers without blinking.

Matt had only met him once, a brisk handshake in the break room, but office talk painted him as Summit's fixer, the man brought in to impose order. The legacy staff all seemed unnerved by him, lowering their voices when he passed.

The fact that he knew Matt's name was unsettling. That he had asked for him specifically was worse.

Matt nodded, throat tight. "Okay. Sure, but this feels like a step backward."

Walking back to his desk, his stomach churned.

Goose. The engine. The code.

For nearly a year, the skimming job had run on its own. He had watched the offshore balance grow like a shadow in the corner of his life, but he hadn't touched it. Not once, and in any case, he couldn't. Access had been taken away.

Now, with this reassignment, everything had changed. Goose system access would be back in his hands. And this created the opportunity for him to kill his skimming code.

That afternoon, the data security team sent him a new Goose development account. This meant a set of credentials that permitted him to modify the system's code, a type of access reserved for trusted developers only. This was the access that had initially allowed him to build the skimming job. It was the primary key to Goose, the door into the heart of the system.

Most employees would never experience this level of privilege, and even fewer were trusted to maintain it. To Matt, the notification felt heavier than a promotion letter. It was permission and temptation bound in one place.

When he was finally in again, his chest tightened. The old thrill of access, the sense of having his hands on the pulse of the company, had returned, but underneath it was dread.

At breakfast the next morning, Bernice watched him push eggs around his plate.

"What's wrong?" she asked.

"Nothing," he blurted. "Just work stuff. They've got me back on Goose with Derek."

Her fork stopped. "That's a step backward." She frowned. "But with Summit in charge ... I guess it makes sense. Just push through. With any luck, you'll be out soon."

She tried to sound steady, but her nails tapped against her mug. Inside, her thoughts churned:

Why does he always shut me out? Why won't he tell me what's eating him?

With the baby coming, she needed him rooted, not drifting. The warmth of the kitchen—toast, coffee, the hum of the heater—did nothing to ease the knot in her stomach.

Matt told himself that he knew exactly what to do—exactly what was right: the new access would allow him to *kill the code.*

Yet the thought didn't come without argument.

In his head, he drew up a list, almost like a balance sheet. On one side: relief, freedom, a clean slate. On the other: risk, potential red flags, and money.

He weighed the logic back and forth until his temples ached. He thought of Bernice's face if it all came crashing down, of the baby's future.

Still, when he let the debate settle, one truth rose above the noise: ending the code was the only way to reclaim himself, to put this to bed. The pros outweighed the cons. He had to kill it, and that was exactly what he was going to do. He imagined standing in the server room, entering the kill command, and walking away lighter. The thought gave him both courage and terror.

THREE DAYS LATER, he was alone in the server room. The air was cool, tinged with dust and hot metal. Fans droned in a steady rhythm. On the terminal, the skimming job blinked up at him like a secret laid bare.

One command, that was all it was going to take.

All he needed to do was delete one file. It would be gone in less than a minute.

Sweat trickled down his back. His fingers hovered over the keys. The thrum of the room pressed in on him. For an instant, he saw himself clearly: not decisive, not in control, but shackled to the thing he had built.

A dome camera blinked above. Petrov's new system recorded every keystroke. Killing the job would leave his fingerprints all over it. He pictured the questions that would follow, the suspicious glances, the email from security.

He pushed back his chair, the scrape loud in the quiet. And he walked out. His pulse running so high, he could feel his heartbeat in his ears.

He hadn't done it. Another week, he told himself. One more chance. He clung to half-baked excuses. The money wasn't the point. He hadn't touched it. But the account had become something else, proof, a scoreboard only he could see. Letting it run felt safer than pulling the plug.

The next day, he took a vacation day. He had scheduled interviews at Nations Bank.

It turned out to be six hours, five different rooms, and the same questions repeated. The air throughout the office smelled of coffee and carpet cleaner, with the HVAC humming overhead. He caught glimpses of other candidates in the waiting area, tense faces clutching folders. The formality of it all reminded him how much he wanted out. By the fourth interview, his answers rolled off his tongue like rehearsed code, steady but desperate.

By the time he stepped outside into the noise of traffic, his pulse was racing. Relief washed through him, almost dizzying. He pulled out his mobile phone and called Bernice right away. She picked up on the second ring. He told her how well it had gone, that he was sure the offer would come.

There was a pause, then her voice warmed with excitement, but also with caution. "That's wonderful, Matt," she said. "If this really happens, maybe we can finally breathe a little easier." Her words steadied him even more than the rush of the interviews. He felt buoyed, almost giddy, as he walked to his car.

Two days later, his computer chimed. He read the email once. Then again. Then again.

Offer confirmed: $100,000 base, bonus eligible, full benefits. Title: Team Lead, Branch Systems; AS/400 Division.

He leaned back in his chair. Relief rushed through him, leaving him lightheaded. He called Bernice again. She answered quickly, and when he told her the news, she laughed and let out a breath, her voice bubbling with excitement but edged with tears. "Matt, that's incredible. We're going to be okay."

Only after hearing her reaction, after feeling that shared moment of release, did he call Ira.

"Congratulations, my friend," Ira said, cheerful as ever. "You deserve this." Matt barely heard the rundown of start dates and background checks. His thoughts were already racing ahead. Tomorrow could be different.

That night, the smell of sesame chicken filled the living room. Bernice curled on the couch, one hand over her belly.

"Are you happy?" she asked.

"I am," he said, and felt it. "Clean slate. New job. New baby. More money."

Her eyes softened. She tapped the letter with her finger. "This feels safer. With the baby coming ... we need this."

Inside, she tried to believe it fully. Still, she remembered his pacing, his silences. She pressed her palm to her stomach. It has to change—for all our sakes. She wondered if the new job would anchor him or if the shadows of Goose would follow.

"I'm proud of you," she whispered. "It's time."

That night, Matt lay in the dark, rehearsing his resignation like a script. He pictured the Goose directories, the three lines of code it would take. *Tomorrow,* he promised himself. *Tomorrow, it ends.*

For once, he slept well.

Morning brought frost across lawns and rooftops; the air was biting cold. The kitchen filled with the smell of butter and coffee as he cooked eggs. Bernice shuffled in, robe pulled tight, sipping her decaf.

"You nervous?" she asked.

"A little. But ready."

She studied him, trying to believe it. His face looked lighter. Still, doubt lingered at the edges. She sipped her coffee and thought of the bills stacked on the counter, the baby clothes folded in the spare room, the uncertainty that clung to them. She smiled anyway.

At the office, a few early risers tapped at keyboards. Matt walked straight to Rajive's office, resignation letter folded in his pocket.

Rajive read it silently, then set it down. "I was expecting this. Surprised it didn't come sooner."

Matt frowned. "Really?"

"You've been halfway out for months," Rajive said. "Not sloppy, but distant. I noticed."

Matt managed a small smile. "Didn't think it showed."

"Not to most. But I pay attention." Rajive leaned back,

fingers steepled. "You're going to be a dad. You want stability. This place isn't that anymore."

Matt swallowed. "I appreciate everything you've done."

"I know." Rajive stood. "No need to drag it out. We'll make it effective today. HR will sort the rest. The company will pay you throughout the notice period."

Matt blinked. "Wow, that was fast?"

"Better for everyone. You've got a future waiting. Go start it."

For a moment, Rajive's eyes lingered. Too long. Matt's chest tightened.

Did he know that his chance to kill the code was slipping away?

Within minutes, HR shut down his access. Goose. Email. Everything gone. The swift action stunned him, as if someone had erased his entire working life with the flick of a switch. His stomach dropped.

When he walked back through the open-plan office, the familiar chatter and clatter of keyboards felt strangely distant. A few colleagues looked up, some curious, others avoiding his eyes. He forced a nod to one or two of them, but no words came. He noticed Kelly from operations glance quickly away, and Pete from accounting gave him a sympathetic half-smile, but no one spoke.

Back at his desk, Derek was there, calm as ever, sipping coffee. Matt searched his face for recognition, some sign of shared history with Goose, but Derek only gave a brief, unreadable glance before turning back to his screen. The silence between them pressed heavier than words.

He boxed a few photos, a mug, a couple of books. By the time he walked out, his badge no longer opened the door. The final click of the lock left him cold.

Matt felt it was strange that Summit hadn't asked him for system documentation. Their controls were weaker than SBF's ever were. They were more focused on cutting corners in the name of speed and greater profits.

At a stoplight near Marietta Square, Matt paused on his way to savor the smell of roasted peanuts drifting through his window.

Was he doing the right thing?

Should he be leaving SBF—leaving Goose?

Or would this move be the catalyst to bring everything crashing down?

BERNICE'S EYEBROWS rose when he came home early. "You're back?"

"Yep." He set the box on the counter.

"They kicked you out?"

"Pretty much."

She laughed, shaking her head.

"Good. You're ours now."

She called her office, said she wasn't feeling well, and stayed home. The house filled with cocoa and vanilla candlelight. Cheers reruns played in the background. Bernice lounged under a knit blanket, her belly a full curve beneath her sweater, a mug of cocoa balanced on top.

Matt knelt at her feet, massaging them gently. Laughter came easily as they tossed baby names back and forth, some ridiculous, some rooted in family. For a little while, the weight lifted.

Yet Bernice watched him when he wasn't looking. Would he always be this tender, this present? Or would that faraway stare return? She prayed the new job would ground him, that the shadows from SBF would stay behind.

That night, Matt stared at the ceiling. The resignation was done. Nations was real. But the code still ran. Goose still skimmed. Derek's calmness during outages drifted through his thoughts, chilling him like a draft.

He pulled out his laptop and checked the Antigua account.

$254,670.20.

Still growing. Still untouched.

Untouchable now, even to him.

He was free from the company. But not of the code.

He should have ended it. Why hadn't he?

As he lay in the darkness, he struggled to find the right answer. He had had the opportunity to end this nightmare and, for whatever reason, had failed to take it.

In his mind, he saw the balance ticking upward, digit by digit. Alive ... a thing he had set loose, pulsing in the dark, and now forever beyond his reach.

CHAPTER 30
ALFIE

T hree full weeks before her due date, in the soft quiet of a Thursday morning, Bernice shook Matt awake at 3:14 a.m. with a groan and a look he would never forget. Her hand gripped his wrist like a vice.

"It's happening."

They scrambled.

They had not yet packed the hospital bag. Matt rushed around while Bernice gave directions, her voice breaking into gasps, her hand waving toward the dresser and then toward the door. His shoes squeaked on the hardwood as he darted between rooms, muttering half-finished sentences. "Keys— where the hell ... bag—did you ..." Bernice clutched the door-frame, pale, biting her lip, trying to stay composed, her eyes wide with panic.

Finally, they were in the car, en route to the hospital. The timing, the car ride, the calls to her parents, to Nations—it all felt frantic. Nations had already given him the green light to duck out when the baby arrived, but because everything was happening so suddenly, and ahead of schedule, he wanted to give them a heads-up.

Matt hit the gas pedal as rain slicked the asphalt. The headlights cut narrow tunnels through the mist. Bernice pressed her forehead against the cold glass between contractions, silently praying their little one would be safe.

When they arrived at the Cobb County WellStar Hospital maternity ward, the smell of disinfectant hit them immediately —sharp, sterile, almost metallic. Fluorescent lights hummed above, bleaching the hallway walls a dull white. Bernice winced with another contraction, gripping Matt's sleeve so hard he nearly dropped the paperwork. Her parents met them at the intake area, faces flushed with excitement and worry. Bernice caught her mother's eye and, for a fleeting second, wanted to collapse into her arms like a child, but the pain reminded her she had crossed that line for good—she was the mother now.

The hours blurred. There was pain, gas, laughter, nurses. The squeak of rubber soles echoed with each urgent step. A faint lullaby played over the hospital intercom, announcing a birth elsewhere, just as Bernice bit down on a scream.

"You've got this, honey, breathe," Matt whispered, brushing damp hair from her forehead, his voice breaking though he tried to sound steady. She was astonishing, resolute, fierce, funny even in her agony—though inside she wrestled with panic, whispering to herself that she couldn't do this, that she wasn't ready, until each contraction forced her body to prove otherwise. At 10:28 a.m., she gave one final push, and their son was born.

Five pounds, four ounces. A little red, a little squashed, but alive and beautiful. They named him Alfie.

Bernice wept softly as they laid him on her chest. She kissed his damp hair, whispering promises he would never remember, but she would never forget: she would always protect him, she would always be there. Matt stood there, stunned and overwhelmed. His eyes stung as he tried to absorb the moment: the beeping of monitors, the shuffle of medical staff, the muffled cry of his new son. Somewhere beneath the flood of emotion and adrenaline, he thought about how none of this felt real, and yet, it was the most real thing he'd ever known.

They stayed in the hospital for several nights, doctors keeping a close watch because Alfie had arrived early. Bernice's recovery was uncomplicated, though she quietly worried over every sound Alfie made, checking his chest for the rise and fall of breath even as nurses reassured her.

Fortunately, Alfie thrived in the nursery. By the end of the weekend, a nurse wheeled her down to the curb, holding Alfie in a blanket the color of robins' eggs. Bernice held Alfie's little hand the entire ride home as she sat next to his car seat, irrationally afraid Matt might hit a pothole too hard.

At home, life detonated.

Matt thought he would be prepared.

He wasn't.

The crying, the feedings, the fear that something, anything, might go wrong. He barely slept. Bernice, to her credit, was calm and steady. She struggled with the same exhaustion but powered through it, often whispering to herself at 3 a.m., "If he sleeps, I can sleep. Just one hour. One blessed hour."

The bedroom smelled of talcum powder, sour milk, and lavender lotion. Her mother stayed with them for the first few days, filling the kitchen with the aroma of casseroles and cornbread and rocking the baby between naps. Matt's parents arrived three days later, beaming with pride, already arguing over which features Alfie had inherited from which side of the family.

Bernice smiled at them, but sometimes she felt invisible inside, as if the child had replaced her in everyone's eyes. She loved Alfie fiercely, but part of her longed for someone to ask how she was doing, beyond the polite medical check-ins. And beneath it all, she noticed Matt's silences more, storing them away as questions she never voiced.

It was chaos, but chaos filled with immeasurable joy. And Matt, for the first time in a long time, let go of the guilt. For a while, at least.

A week later, on a drizzly Monday morning, Matt walked into the Midtown regional office of Nations Bank for his first day. Rain streaked the windows and pooled in the cracked sidewalks outside. He wore a sharp new suit and carried a new notebook, the paper still stiff. A reusable mug filled with his favorite Dunkin' Donuts coffee went untouched, the steam fading as he adjusted his tie. His mind was still half back at home, picturing Bernice's weary smile and the tiny rise and fall of Alfie's chest. But he was also ready. Ready for a reset. Ready to start over.

His new office was clean and corporate, with gray walls, modular furniture, and a decent window that framed a skyline shrouded in drizzle. The team he led maintained legacy AS/400 systems used by retail branch operations across five southeastern states. When his new manager stopped by with a perfunctory handshake and a "Good to have you," Matt smiled politely, his grip firm but his mind elsewhere. It was unglamorous work, but steady. Reliable.

Matt welcomed the routine.

The days settled in quickly. Bernice returned to work after 10 weeks of maternity leave, and Alfie started attending a small day nursery near Bernice's office. Every morning was a symphony of feeding, dressing, packing, and racing to beat Atlanta traffic. Horns blared, wipers beat time against the windshield. Every evening brought bottles, laundry, and lots of yawns.

On her way home from work, Bernice often drove with the radio off, alone with her thoughts, wondering whether she was giving enough to both her job and her son and fearing she was failing at both. Some nights she looked at Matt, grateful for his steady paycheck, but unsettled by the way his gaze drifted past her, as though he were watching something only he could see.

One night, after putting Alfie down, Bernice curled beside Matt on the couch and said with a tired smile, "I'm just glad Nations feels steady. No surprises. We can finally breathe." She tucked her feet under her, reaching for his hand.

He gave it a squeeze but kept his eyes fixed on the muted television, the flicker of light playing across his face. The soft lamplight painted the room gold as she rested her head on his shoulder, trusting. Inside, though, she wondered if the faraway look in his eyes would ever disappear.

But amid all the normalcy, the old itch returned.

The next day, as he sat at his desk, he checked the Antigua account. He had not planned to ever log in to that account again. He told himself he was done with it. But during a quiet period, he caved in, opened the browser, and logged on.

$612,016.10.

His breath caught.

The skimming code was still alive. Still working.

Business must be booming.

His stomach tightened. At this velocity, any glitch, any stray log entry, could draw attention. It no longer felt like safe money. It felt volatile.

He sat back in his chair, unsettled. His hand lingered on the receiver, hesitation prickling. Part of him wanted to call Bernice, to confess the number staring back at him, but he knew she would hear it as a threat to the fragile calm they'd built. So instead, he almost reflexively called Rajive.

"Matt! Look at you, calling from your big bank tower," Rajive answered, his voice warm and teasing. Matt forced a laugh, rolling the cord between his fingers. They talked briefly, Rajive rattling off the pressures at Summit while Matt interjected with polite nods and was a little distracted, as his eyes fixed on the account balance still glowing on his screen.

Back at home, Bernice noticed the distance in his voice when they spoke that evening. She sensed he was holding something back. "Long day?" she asked softly, brushing her hair behind one ear.

Matt kissed her cheek, a mechanical peck, and muttered, "Just tired."

Why won't he tell me what's really on his mind? She thought, replaying the half-hearted way he described his day. *Is Nations not what he hoped, or is it something else?* That night, she lay awake long after Matt fell asleep, staring at the ceiling, turning over the possibilities. Each theory unsettled her more, but she swallowed them in silence.

When he got home the following evening, he went directly to the nursery and stared at his sleeping son. The night-light glowed amber against the pale blue walls, casting soft shadows over the stuffed animals lined neatly on a shelf. Bernice leaned in the doorway, watching him, her own thoughts tumbling.

He looks at Alfie as if the entire world is on his shoulders. What is he carrying that he won't tell me? She wrapped her arms around herself, torn between giving him space and demanding answers.

Alfie sighed in his sleep and curled slightly, tiny fists bunched under his chin. The faint scent of baby powder and warm milk hung in the air. Matt closed his eyes. A fierce surge of love and dread collided in his chest. How could he protect this child if his long-held secret could explode at any moment?

He should have shut it down. Why didn't he stop it when he had the chance?

The Antigua balance ticked in his imagination, digits climbing like sparks racing along a wire. It didn't feel like a secret anymore. It felt like a fuse.

Bernice felt it too—the undercurrent she had never been able to name. She pressed her cheek to the doorframe, whispering a silent plea that whatever haunted him would not tear them apart. Part of her wanted to step into the room, to press him to talk, to demand the truth. Another part held back, afraid of what might spill out if she pushed too hard. In that moment, she promised herself that she would protect Alfie from whatever storm Matt carried inside. As she tiptoed back down the hall, she promised herself she would not ignore her instincts again.

CHAPTER 31
SUNSET CODE

A year passed. It was the summer of 1999, and the world buzzed with nervous anticipation of the new millennium. At Nations Bank, Matt worked in the trenches of Y2K testing. Every legacy system was under scrutiny; every line of COBOL was combed through in the hunt for rogue two-digit year fields.

His days stretched long and meticulous, but there was satisfaction in the grind. The work felt purposeful, almost noble—a collective mission to prevent chaos, to make sure the world's ATMs kept working when the calendar rolled over.

The Midtown office carried the weight of tradition. The lobby smelled vaguely of polished wood and carpet cleaner, a place where whispers traveled farther than intended. Elevators chimed dully and opened onto floors that seemed cut from the same gray cloth.

Matt's division was tucked away on the seventh floor, a maze of cubicles where each space told its own story, with curling Y2K checklists, Dilbert cartoons faded from sunlight, and mugs brought back from long-forgotten vacations. The air carried the constant smell of burnt coffee from the break room pot that never quite came clean.

Matt's own office was narrow but private, a rectangle of gray walls and a desk facing a window onto Peachtree Street and a skyline view. Some days, he cracked the pane to let in muffled city sounds—horns, bus brakes, the occasional street saxophone. On quiet afternoons, the low rumble of MARTA trains rattled the glass, an urban heartbeat beneath his work.

The culture was steady but cautious. Posters about Y2K readiness dotted the walls—some grim, others joking: *Don't Let Two Digits Ruin Your Life.* Printers hummed, keyboards tapped in steady rhythm, and the gurgle of the water cooler punctuated the background drone. Compared to SBF, this was order, even if at times the sameness pressed down on him.

His colleagues filled the place with personality.

Harris, the fifty-something analyst with oatmeal bowls and coffee-stained ties, lived for the manual binders stacked around him. Priya, a sharp coder from Emory with a desk lined with neon sticky notes like confetti, smiled easily and spotted bugs no one else caught. Gordon, the team joker, taped fresh millennium bug cartoons to monitors each Friday. They weren't glamorous, but they were reliable. For Matt, reliability was a kind of salvation.

Downstairs, the trading floor roared like another planet. Phones rang nonstop, traders barked orders, and glowing screens spilled light across sweating faces. The air reeked of cologne, coffee, and the metallic bite of overheated electronics. Matt rarely had reason to be there, and when he did, he always left with his ears ringing, grateful to retreat upstairs where the worst threat was a misplaced semicolon.

Jokes about planes dropping from the sky or elevators freezing mid-floor carried through the office, laughter edged with nerves. Matt smiled along, hiding the truth they would never guess somewhere, code he had written still lived in Goose, quietly drawing dollars away. That shadow was his alone.

At home, life drowned out some of the unease. Alfie was nearly walking, wobbling on stout legs and laughing as he turned pots into drums. At Coca-Cola, Bernice was balancing motherhood and work with a grace that cracked only behind the bathroom door when she thought no one could hear. Matt tried to be steady—bottle in one hand, Alfie in the other.

Bernice whispered encouragement to herself during late-night feeds: *One more bottle, one more night.* Driving to the daycare each morning, she sometimes wondered if she was holding everything together or just faking it well. Matt's eyes drifted even when Alfie clutched his finger, and she noticed it. She told herself it was work fatigue, but in her gut, she knew it was heavier. She held back from asking, afraid that pressing too hard might crack their fragile peace.

Still, Matt couldn't let go of the offshore account. Every few months, long after Bernice had gone to bed and Alfie's room had fallen silent, he crept into the study and logged in. The monitor's glow lit his face as the number appeared.

$2,147,602.40.

It stunned him every time—part wonder, part dread. The balance had swollen like a wound left untended. He hadn't touched Goose, hadn't written a single new line. Yet the account climbed.

Sometimes he sat frozen for half an hour, weighing confession against ruin. He pictured Bernice at the kitchen table, hearing the truth, her eyes hardening. He imagined calling a lawyer, his chest tight with images of headlines and prison gates. Each scenario ended in disaster. So, he chose silence, again and again.

He told himself it would fade. Systems were retired, and the code would soon diminish from his memory. One day, the deposits would stop, the balance would freeze, and he could pretend it had never happened.

Then one night, it did.

The account showed the same figure as the month before.
$2,147,602.40.
Not a cent higher.
He refreshed. Waited. Refreshed again. Nothing moved.
Sweat gathered on his palms.

Was it frozen? Flagged? Found?

That night, he lay awake, staring at the ceiling, hearing every creak of the house as an accusation.

This is it. They know. They're coming.

Beside him, Bernice stirred, but she simply rolled away, whispering incoherently. Matt sighed in relief. He couldn't face her in this state.

By morning, Matt's nerves had knotted tight. He dialed Rajive.

The old number still worked. Relief flooded him when Rajive answered on the second ring, his voice familiar and warm.

"Matt! Long time."

"Hey, Raj. Got a minute?"

"Always. How's life treating you?"

They traded updates about families and work. Rajive was still at SBF, now under Summit Funding Partners, his humor intact but wearied.

"I hear you're buried in Project 2000," Matt said carefully.

"Oh yeah. Summit finally decided Goose couldn't scale forever, so they kicked off a migration. Consultants everywhere, diagrams on every wall. It's a circus, but they're paying for it."

Matt's throat went dry. "So, Goose is gone?"

Rajive chuckled. "Not yet. It's a hybrid. Summit upgraded hardware, but most of Goose's code got reused or rewritten by Derek. Some jobs still run on Goose while others shift to Eagle, the shiny new system. They expect to complete the cutover in six months. Funny thing is that parts of Goose impressed them.

Especially the batch scheduling. Called it elegant. Your work still shows."

Matt couldn't help but feel a twinge of pride.

Rajive continued. "Eagle's live in parts, but Goose is still critical. Derek's been the linchpin—they even gave him a big bonus. In the break room, Derek joked about 'retiring the haunted hour.' No one asked which ghost he meant."

Matt forced a laugh. "End of an era, I guess."

"Tell me about it," Rajive said. "Old beast served us, but it's time."

When the call ended, Matt sat staring at his phone. He reopened the account. Same number.

$2,147,602.40.

The digits glowed, flat and unchanging.

For years, the balance had been his secret scoreboard, a fuse sparking in the dark. Now it was static. Relief flickered, chased by loss.

Was this freedom or another trap?

He thought of Square Consulting LLC, still registered in Antigua.

Would shutting it bury the trail or spotlight it?

Some nights, he drafted letters in his head, confessions to Bernice, apologies she would find after he was gone. By dawn, the words had dissolved, and he buried the guilt again.

The money sat in his mind not as wealth but as waste—sealed, glowing, still toxic.

One night, as Matt lay awake, rolling the money over and over in his mind, he heard Alfie's soft cry from the nursery. The innocent sound cut him to the core. He closed his eyes, caught between two worlds, but he pushed down his dread, pushed down everything that kept him from connecting with what mattered most: Alfie.

In his nursery, Matt scooped up the boy and hugged him tight. Alfie squealed with delight.

Bernice, who hadn't been far behind Matt, lingered in the hallway, watching. Pride and love swelled as Matt held their son, but her ever-present unease sharpened as she once again saw the faraway look on his face.

What storm is he hiding from us? She wondered, hugging herself. She vowed to keep watch, to trust her instincts.

It should have been over. He wanted to believe it was. But nothing that large, that unnatural, ever vanished cleanly.

CHAPTER 32
SHOCK

F ive years had passed. Now, in mid-2004, Matt Hall found his life in a rhythm that he could only describe as successful. He had climbed the ranks at Nations Bank and now sat atop the trading room application development division as its global head. A team of 30 technologists reported to him, and his name appeared on more and more executive meeting invites. His title carried weight, and with it came a generous compensation package, equity options, and the constant, subtle pressure to relocate to the company's head office in Charlotte.

At home, things had never been better. He and Bernice now had three children: Alfie, their spirited oldest; Stella, a precocious toddler with her mother's curls; and baby Mark, who had just celebrated his first birthday. Their townhouse on Cole Street, once the perfect starter home, was now bursting at the seams. Toys lined the staircase, sippy cups cluttered the sink, and storage bins overflowed with outgrown baby clothes. The couple had begun discussing selling their home and moving to a larger place, perhaps in Buckhead or Sandy Springs. Alongside that came talk of private school options, bigger mortgages, and higher daycare costs—money pressure that made Matt's stomach tighten whenever Bernice casually raised it.

Matt hadn't thought about the Antigua account in years. Not really. Sure, the monthly paper statements still arrived in the mail. He'd made no effort to cancel them, but they went straight into the shredder, unopened. It had become a ritual. By refusing to look, he could convince himself it didn't exist. He had long ago learned how to compartmentalize, and this had brought him relief.

For years now, he had come to terms with what he'd done. In his mind, it wasn't a crime. He had written a piece of code, an intellectual exercise. He had never withdrawn a cent, never moved the funds, never spent the money. The account had become a digital ghost—there, but untouched. He told himself that he had proven a point: that one could beat the system if clever enough.

Then, unexpectedly, came the article that would bring back the old pain, the old anxieties.

It was a Thursday morning, late July. Matt had a cup of Dunkin' Donuts hazelnut coffee in his hand as he idly flipped through the *Wall Street Journal* in his office before his first meeting. The headline caught his eye:

Silver Thatch Financial to Acquire Summit Funding Partners in $1.2 Billion Deal.

His eyes froze. Silver Thatch. A Cayman Islands hedge fund with a reputation for ruthless cost-cutting and short-term profit extraction. And Summit—still operating publicly under the SBF name, still running large parts of the Goose code at its core.

A strange unease crept into his chest. He read the article in full. They planned to close the deal in the fall. The hedge fund would keep the SBF brand but cut deep into its operating costs. They would merge the US offices, significantly reduce staff, and review systems for "efficiency gains."

That last line remained in his mind: "We have no plans for any major IT investments in the near future."

He wasn't sure why, but something in his gut told him to check—just one last time.

That evening at home, his nerves showed. During dinner, Alfie asked him if he was sick. Bernice gave him a long, pointed look across the table, one that said she wasn't buying his mumbled, "Just work stuff."

Later, once the children were in bed and Bernice was folding laundry upstairs, Matt slipped into his home office. He unlocked the filing cabinet, pulled out the old backup drive, and connected it to his personal laptop—not his Nations Bank machine. He took precautions, tunneling through a VPN he'd set up years ago, masking his traffic so it looked as if it had originated overseas. Nations was far stricter than SBF had ever been; firewalls, monitoring tools, and audit trails were now part of the culture. Logging in directly from the office network would've been reckless. Even in his own house, his pulse quickened at every click.

There, buried beneath nested folders, was the secure shell app and the bookmark he hadn't touched in nearly five years.

He clicked.

The screen took a moment to load. When it did, his heart lurched.

$18,430,242.50.

His stomach twisted. He felt lightheaded. He pushed away from the desk and stumbled toward the bathroom.

Sweat beaded along his hairline. His temples throbbed. He gripped the edge of the sink and stared at his reflection. His face looked pale, eyes wide, as though someone else's terror stared back at him.

How is this even possible?

The next morning, once he reached the office, he closed his door and picked up the phone to call Rajive, praying he was still at SBF and desperate for an explanation. To Matt's relief, Rajive answered. After a few minutes of polite catching up with families and work, Matt asked carefully, "Raj, whatever happened to Derek? Is he still there?"

There was a pause before Rajive sighed. "Funny you ask. Derek actually led the first phase of the Silver Thatch integration. He copied whole chunks of Goose into the patched-together systems they were rolling out and said it was faster than rewriting everything. Six months later, once things were stable, they cut him loose. Hedge fund logic—no loyalty, just savings." Rajive gave a weary chuckle. "But a lot of Goose logic made it across untouched. Too much, probably. Derek was always too neat with his migrations."

Matt felt his stomach knot. Derek unknowingly must have carried over his embedded skimming code into the hedge fund's operating platform.

Eighteen million dollars.

The figure circled in his head like a vulture. It was more money than he could ever plausibly explain.

If investigators ever saw it, what story could he tell? How does a bank technologist amass $18 million offshore? The thought alone chilled him.

He had never once touched the money. But it had kept growing. And growing. And now, with Silver Thatch's takeover, it might not be long before someone looked. Really looked.

———

THAT NIGHT, Bernice found him sitting in the darkened den. "You, okay?" she asked gently.

He looked up and forced a smile. "Yeah. Just a rough day."

She didn't press, but he saw the doubt in her eyes. A hot pang of guilt lanced through him.

He could never tell her. Not now. Not ever.

The next morning, he arrived at the office before 7:00. He didn't even take off his blazer. Instead, he walked straight to his desk, opened his laptop, and pulled up the international dialing code for Antigua.

He rehearsed his lines. No, he wasn't closing the account. He wasn't transferring funds. He was simply requesting digital rather than paper statements. That was all. Harmless.

He dialed.

After a brief hold, a woman answered.

"Commonwealth Trust Bank of Antigua, good morning."

"Hi, yes," Matt said. "This is Matthew Hall. I have an account at your bank. I'd like to switch from paper statements to online delivery."

"Of course, Mr. Hall. Let me verify a few details."

They went through the usual security questions. She was polite and efficient.

"Okay, sir, I've updated that. You'll no longer receive paper statements. Your online access remains unchanged."

"Perfect. Thank you."

He hung up.

As he set the phone down, another thought stabbed him: had he just reminded them the account existed? In the post-9/11 world, compliance teams were twitchier than ever. A red dot blinking on some AML screen, his name resurfacing after years of silence? He wiped his palms on his blazer, heart hammering.

That was it. His decision was final. He wouldn't log in again. He would delete the secure shell access, scrub the credentials, and wipe the drive. And perhaps, finally, close Square Consulting LLC itself, though the thought unsettled him. Could it ever truly vanish from registries and databases, or would the act of dissolution only leave another scar of evidence? Either way, the account would remain untouched.

He had stolen nothing. Not really. He had never spent a dime. In his mind, that distinction mattered.

But deep inside, as he shut the lid of his laptop and leaned back in his chair, he knew the clock was ticking. It was simply too much money to remain invisible. Even if he burned every trace, the balance still sat out there, compounding like a secret he could never erase.

He was the custodian of a digital time bomb.

And he prayed it would never detonate—not just for him, but for Bernice and the kids.

CHAPTER 33
FINAL ECHO

They moved in mid-April, just as the dogwoods in North Carolina began to bloom. The house they chose was in Myers Park, a quiet, upscale Charlotte neighborhood of winding roads, mature oaks, and stately homes. Their new colonial-style five-bedroom, with white trim and navy shutters, sat at the end of a cul-de-sac. The backyard had a wooden playset and space for a garden. Bernice fell in love on their second visit; Matt hesitated but eventually admitted this was where their future could take root.

Nations Bank made it easy. The relocation package covered the sale of the Atlanta townhouse, movers, and six months of tuition and nursery fees. They even assigned a relocation officer to walk them through schools, neighborhoods, and mortgage options. Matt joked that it felt like a corporate adoption. Bernice smiled but didn't disagree.

He had resisted the move at first. Charlotte seemed distant from Bernice's parents, their friends, and the familiar rhythms of Marietta Square. But the opportunity was too good to refuse. As head of trading room application development, he now oversaw 35 technologists spread across the U.S., London, and Hong Kong. It was the kind of job that came with stock options, corner offices, and a six-figure bonus. More importantly, it gave him the structured stability he craved after the chaos of SBF.

The family settled quickly. Alfie started fourth grade, lanky and restless, his sandy hair always falling into eyes that sparkled with mischief. He was curious about everything, a boy who took apart toys just to see how they worked, and he thrived in classrooms where teachers could channel his energy. Stella, all curls and wide brown eyes, joined a preschool. She was more cautious than her brother, but endlessly imaginative, prone to inventing elaborate games and talking to her dolls as if they were old friends. Baby Mark, too young for school, toddled about the house with a fearless determination that kept Bernice on her toes. Bernice herself found a gym with childcare and made friends on hikes through Crowders Mountain and in carpool lines.

Matt dove into headquarters life, learning the rhythms of Nations Bank's hierarchy and the art of navigating corporate politics. He watched who spoke in meetings, who listened, who held influence through silence. He realized he wasn't just a technologist anymore—he was being groomed as an executive. Some nights, he returned home exhausted but oddly exhilarated, replaying the day's encounters like chess matches.

Bernice felt both pride and loss. She put her own career on hold to focus on the children. At night, folding laundry in the quiet kitchen, she sometimes wondered if she would ever reclaim the ambitions she'd set aside. At Coca-Cola, she once dreamed of climbing the ladder to the top, but now she juggled carpools, pediatric visits, and silent dinners when Matt was late. When he was there, she watched him, his eyes elsewhere, and feared they were drifting into parallel lives.

By summer, their house buzzed with life. Stella learned to ride a bike in the cul-de-sac. Mark, barely two, toddled after her. Bernice planted herbs in the garden and hosted a Fourth of July barbecue under strings of lights, with neighbors crowding the yard, sharing stories and laughter. Matt poured drinks, smiled on cue, but Bernice noticed his gaze wandering, his silences growing heavier. It pained her, though she said nothing.

ONE NIGHT, as Matt flew a red-eye back from a conference in Chicago, a headline in the *Wall Street Journal* jolted him:

Silver Thatch Partners Completes Summit Funding Integration.

His fingers stiffened. He folded the paper, slid it into his bag, and stared out the window for the rest of the flight.

Later, in the early-morning hours when the sun had yet to reappear and the house remained quiet, Matt pulled out the hidden external hard drive, used an encrypted dial-up connection with a proxy server, and logged into the offshore portal with the caution of a man stealing from his own shadow.

$20,432,160.70.

The number had grown. Again.

Cold sweat pricked his skin. He staggered to the bathroom and splashed water on his face, gripping the sink. Seven years without touching the code, without a single withdrawal—yet here it was, still siphoning. Twenty million dollars—a fortune he dared not touch. His reflection in the mirror seemed foreign, guilty eyes staring back at him.

Old fears he thought he had buried stirred again. For years, he had convinced himself he was past the guilt, that time had dulled its edge. Yet, seeing the figure again brought the weight back, pressing hard on his chest. He had lived with the secret so long it had almost become normal, but in that moment, he felt the old panic rise—the thought of discovery, of Bernice learning the truth, of his children someday knowing. Silence had been his refuge, but now it felt like complicity all over again.

The next day, he drifted through work like a ghost. At dinner, Bernice studied him carefully. Later that night, he lay awake, staring at the ceiling, running through desperate options: confess to Bernice, call the authorities, return the funds anonymously, donate it all. He walked through each one in detail, but every path collapsed under fear—prison, scandal, shame. He told himself that inaction was safer, yet imagining alternatives deepened his guilt. And each option, he realized, wasn't just about him. If investigators came, Bernice would have to go through hearings and interviews, and his children would be forced to live under a shadow they could not escape. The very thought of Alfie or Stella facing questions at school about their father being a criminal made him ill.

Some nights, he pictured setting up a charitable trust, funneling the money into hospitals or scholarships, as if good deeds could erase his crime. But even in fantasy, he could not explain the source. No explanation could ever shield Bernice or the children from the stain of scandal. His silence was not only about protecting himself—it had become a fragile barrier holding back shame and ruin from the people he loved most.

By morning, he had convinced himself to try a different plan. He would close Square Consulting LLC, then call Antigua to change the address to a false one in Los Angeles. Risky, maybe reckless, but it felt like action. As he toyed with the idea in his head, he knew it was flimsy—closing the LLC would never erase old filings, and compliance teams loved sniffing around dissolved entities. Changing the address might buy him distance, or it might flag the account for review.

Even silence carried risk; he pictured an investigator someday tracing the untouched balance back to him. Yet, the thought of doing nothing felt worse. He had already switched to online-only access, and he told himself that if he never logged in again, maybe it would wither in silence. It was self-deception, and he knew it, but clinging to the illusion of control was easier than facing the truth.

He made the call. After a long hold, they transferred him twice before he reached a clerk with a soft Antiguan accent. She asked probing questions, put him on hold again to "check with compliance," and returned with additional verifications he hadn't expected. His voice shook as he answered, terrified she would sense something was off. Finally, after what felt like an interrogation, she confirmed the change. Matt hung up, exhausted, his shirt damp with sweat. He closed the Gmail account linked to the bank, but relief never came.

When he set the phone down, his palms were damp. In a post-Patriot Act world, he knew banks were under pressure to prove they knew exactly who their clients were. Anti-money laundering and Know Your Customer rules meant that even something as small as an address change could be logged, reviewed, and escalated by the bank. He imagined a compliance officer watching a queue of alerts scroll across their monitor, his name suddenly appearing among them.

Had he just reminded them that the account existed?

Was his identity now blinking red on some screen in a back office, waiting for a closer look?

The possible consequences spiraled in his mind. If the bank investigated, if regulators called, the first knock on the door would not just endanger him—it would shatter Bernice's trust, turn their children's lives upside down, and stain their family name. He pictured the home they had built in Myers Park, suddenly feeling like a stage set ready to be dismantled, neighbors whispering, Bernice carrying shame she did not deserve, the children marked by a secret they had never chosen. The weight of it pressed down harder than the money ever had.

Weeks passed without incident. The house filled with warmth—Stella pedaled around the cul-de-sac, Mark chased her, and Bernice laughed with neighbors under string lights.

Yet she often caught Matt's distracted stare. "You, okay?" she asked softly. He always nodded. She never looked convinced. Sometimes she lay awake, wondering what shadow he carried, fearing it would one day consume them all.

One night, curiosity overcame fear. He logged in again, his proxy masking the trail.

$20,432,160.70.

No change. Relief mixed with unease. A month later, he checked again. Still no change. And another month. The same.

Had it stopped? Had Silver Thatch's slash-and-burn tactics broken the chain? Or was silence just another kind of danger? Lying awake beside Bernice, listening to the ceiling fan, he wondered if he had escaped—or if the ghost was only waiting to rise again.

CHAPTER 34
SURPRISE KNOCK

The winter sunlight slanted through the kitchen windows, pale and weak, catching the steam curling from a pot of pasta on the stove. The air smelled of tomatoes and garlic. Bernice stood at the counter, guiding Stella as she filled in the bright pages of a workbook. Across the room, Alfie chased Mark with a plastic lightsaber, the smack of plastic on cushions and Mark's squeals of delight cutting through the usual hum of the house. The Myers Park home, often a haven of calm domestic rhythm, buzzed now with the joyful chaos of early evening.

Then came the knock at the door.

Three sharp raps. Firm. Official.

Bernice's head snapped up. "Matt? Are you expecting anyone?"

Matt had just come down the stairs, his tie loosened, a stack of papers from the office in his hand. The sound froze him mid-step. His stomach dropped, a cold coil tightening in his gut. He wasn't expecting anyone. Certainly not this.

He set the papers down, forced a neutral smile at Bernice, and walked to the door. Through the beveled glass, he saw them: two men in dark coats, standing straight, posture deliberate, hands clasped in front.

Federal.

Instinct told him before the badges even came out.

"Mr. Hall?" The taller one, square-jawed, early 40s, held up his credentials. "Special Agent Donnelly, FBI. This is Agent Meyers. May we come in?"

Bernice drifted behind him, a dish towel clutched in her hands. Her eyes darted between Matt and the men. "FBI?" she whispered. A rush of dread ran through her. She thought of the children in the next room, of how quickly their ordinary evening had tilted into something frightening. Questions collided in her head:

What could Matt possibly be involved in? Why was the FBI here? And how long had he kept whatever secret this was from her?

Matt's mouth was dry. "Of course," he managed. He stepped aside, his pulse pounding, every nerve in his body alert. He wondered if the agents could see the sweat beading at his collar.

The agents took seats in the living room, Donnelly on the sofa, Meyers in the armchair. Matt sat opposite them. Bernice lingered in the doorway, arms folded, her eyes fixed on her husband. The atmosphere in the room changed; even the kids sensed it. Alfie's laughter died down, Stella clung to her mother's leg, and Mark tugged at her sweater with wide eyes. Bernice bent down and sent them upstairs with gentle promises of dessert later, though her voice was tight and abrupt.

Donnelly opened a leather folder and clicked his pen, the sound sharp in the silence. "Mr. Hall, we appreciate you speaking with us on short notice. We're investigating financial irregularities originating at Sunbelt Business Funding, later acquired by Summit Funding Partners. You worked there in the mid-90s, correct?"

Matt forced a nod. "Yes. Developer. 94 to 98."

"That matches our records," Donnelly said evenly. "We've uncovered evidence of unauthorized processes embedded in the Goose system. We understand you worked on that platform?" Matt nodded again. "The activity persisted for nearly a decade, diverting fractions of transactions into unauthorized accounts. By our estimates, the total diverted exceeds 24 million dollars."

When Matt heard the amount, his chest clenched so tight he thought his heart might give out.

Matt gripped his knees to hide the trembling of his hands.

Twenty-four million.

His pulse thundered in his ears.

Does that include mine? Or is this in addition?

His mind reeled.

Donnelly's tone stayed calm, almost casual. "The evidence points to a senior developer named Derek Collins. Do you recall him?"

"Yes," Matt said carefully. "Derek was ... one of the veterans. Knew Goose better than anyone."

"That's consistent with what we've gathered," Donnelly replied. "We believe Collins built and maintained the unauthorized routines beginning in the early 90s. They carried forward through the Summit acquisition, and it was only after Silver Thatch Partners took control and stripped down reporting processes that the discrepancies became impossible to ignore."

Meyers leaned forward, his voice low. "We haven't located the funds. It seems Collins concealed them offshore. All internal payment accounts had been scrubbed. But we were able to determine through the Wells Fargo account that the money had been sent to a bank in Antigua, but frankly, both the bank and the local authorities there refuse to cooperate. That's part of what brings us here; we're speaking with former colleagues to better understand his methods."

Matt's tongue felt heavy. He nodded, answering questions in clipped, cautious phrases.

Derek had been secretive, yes.

Derek often worked alone.

The system was messy; no one knew it all.

He gave them what was safe, what was expected. Inside, his chest burned with the thought:

Twenty-four million. My twenty million sits out there, too. Are they counting it together? Or are there two shadows?

The agents scribbled their notes. Donnelly closed the folder at last. "Thank you, Mr. Hall. You've been helpful. To be clear, you are not a suspect. This is background. If we need anything further, we'll be in touch."

They rose, shook his hand, and left with the same professional calm they had carried in with them.

The door clicked shut. For a long moment, the house was silent. Matt stood frozen, staring at the door as if it might open again. His shirt clung damp to his back.

Behind him, Bernice's voice cut through the silence, sharp and trembling. "Matt. What the hell was that?"

He turned slowly. She stood rigid, arms crossed, her eyes blazing with fear and accusation. "FBI agents. In our home. Talking about millions of dollars of fraud. Why were they here? Why were they talking to you?"

Matt opened his mouth, then closed it again. He searched for words, for something that would calm her without betraying him. "I ... I worked there. Back then. They're investigating an old colleague. They just wanted context."

Bernice's jaw tightened. "And you didn't think to tell me any of this? That you might get dragged into an investigation?"

"I didn't know," Matt said quickly, too quickly. "I swear I didn't know."

She stared at him, searching his face. "You looked terrified."

Matt swallowed. "Because FBI agents showed up unannounced. Anyone would be."

Her eyes lingered doubtfully. Memories of past silences, his distant stares, pressed against her chest like proof she had ignored for years. But she said nothing more. She turned away and called the kids back down, her movements sharp. Her voice was tight as she soothed them into their routines. Plates clinked, the smell of pasta filled the kitchen again, but an icy gulf had opened between them.

Later that night, with the children asleep, Bernice confronted him again. She sat on the edge of the bed, arms folded. "Matt, if there's something you need to tell me, now is the time."

He shook his head, heart hammering. "There isn't. They were here about Derek. That's all."

She studied him for a long time, then looked away, lips pressed tight. "I hope you're telling me the truth. For all our sakes." But her mind continued to race with questions she didn't dare ask:

What if this shadow swallowed them whole?

What would be the children's fate if their father were caught in a scandal?

She lay awake long after turning out the light, staring at the ceiling, her trust in Matt eroding with every unanswered doubt.

Matt stayed at the window, staring out at the quiet street. His reflection looked back, pale and drawn. His mind churned.

Derek had built a skimming agent—10 years, 24 million, hidden offshore—undiscovered until now. The revelation should have brought Matt relief, proof that someone else was the architect of the fraud. But instead, it twisted tighter inside him. Derek's scheme was not a separate shadow; it overlapped his own in eerie ways, both of them feeding on the same system, both hidden in plain sight. They had never conspired, never spoken of such things, yet Matt felt as though parallel sins bound them.

In his darker moments, he wondered if the investigators would ever believe they had acted independently. Side by side, their ghosts looked like a conspiracy. Derek had been meticulous, sometimes too meticulous, poring over log files with an intensity that unsettled Matt even back then. He remembered Derek's sidelong glances, the quiet questions about modules Matt had touched, as though piecing together a puzzle he never spoke of.

Had Derek suspected Matt's ghost?

Was his silence all those years a cover, or even a trap? The FBI couldn't trace it, but what if Derek had? What if, before his fall, he had whispered hints to someone else, leaving a trail that might one day reach Matt?

But what about his own? His 20 million still sat frozen, unclaimed, a ghost in Antigua. Was it part of Derek's total? Or would another investigation peel back the layers and find his fingerprints, his lines of code still pulsing in a system he no longer controlled?

He closed his eyes, pressing his forehead against the cool glass. Relief should have come; he wasn't the target. Derek was the villain. But relief never came—only dread.

Because if someone found Derek's ghost, what chance did his own have of staying buried forever?

Silence wasn't safety. It was only waiting.

EPILOGUE:
BROWN ENVELOPE

For a while, it seemed as if the world exhaled. The headlines came in a staccato rhythm across the spring and summer: first the arrest, then the indictment, then a steady drumbeat of pretrial filings that the financial press summarized with relish.

Derek Collins, a former senior developer at Sunbelt Business Funding—later Summit Funding Partners operating under the SBF brand, and ultimately under hedge fund ownership by Silver Thatch Partners—stands accused of orchestrating a years-long fraud.

The write-ups were clinical, block quotes from prosecutors, gray-scale photos of a man leaving a courthouse in a too-thin jacket, a face you could project anything onto.

Matt read every line he could find and tried to pretend he wasn't.

At the breakfast table, he kept the paper folded in half and thirds so that Bernice wouldn't see the front page. At the office, he opened articles in a background window and closed them before anyone passed his door. When the television in the trading floor lounge flashed a headline—FORMER DEVEL-OPER IMPLICATED IN MASSIVE SKIMMING CASE—he looked away and poured more coffee he didn't plan on drinking.

The facts, as the world saw them, came into focus. Investigators alleged Collins had inserted unauthorized processes into the Goose system as early as 1993 and kept them alive, in one form or another, through migrations and ownership upheaval.

The scale staggered everyone: roughly $24 million diverted over a decade by shaving slivers from thousands of transactions and whisking them away offshore. The funds themselves were not located—prosecutors emphasized "unknown foreign accounts" and "opaque corporate vehicles."

Collins appeared twice on camera, once walking stone-faced with his lawyer, and once stopping long enough to say, "That number is not possible," before ducking into a black sedan.

After that, he went silent. Negotiations began. The financial press, deprived of fresh quotes, turned to animated timelines and explainers with little pulsing graphics showing pennies splitting and flowing into a glowing blue pool labeled OFFSHORE.

In the end, there was no trial. Collins pleaded guilty to wire fraud and money laundering and was sentenced to 10 years. The authorities found nothing to confiscate. The story slid down the page, then off it. A thing the industry would talk about at conferences for a year and then remember only as a cautionary tale.

For the first time in years, Matt slept. Really slept.

Bernice noticed the difference before he did. He came home less brittle, lingered in the kitchen while the pasta boiled, laughed more easily at Mark's knock-knock jokes. On weekends, he took Stella to the park and timed Alfie around the block on his bike, pretending to lose count when Alfie beat his previous mark by three seconds. In quiet moments, watching his children squabble and then collapse into a pile on the couch, he told himself the story had found its villain and the book had closed.

He wanted to confess to Bernice, but the more he thought about it, the more he persuaded himself not to. He tried to compartmentalize it again.

Still, the thought kept circling back: $20 million ... frozen and waiting somewhere in a server room filled with air he would never breathe, a number that neither grew nor shrank, a seam in the world only he could see. Collins had taken the fall. The sum in the headlines was the government's sum.

What if his money wasn't in it? What if his ghost still lived alone?

Would he be able to get access to the money?

He had considered this many times. He hated the thought, but he fed it. At night, when the house was quiet, and the good whiskey was down to one finger, he would let himself stand on the edge of the idea and look over: a test transfer, tiny, laughable, a rounding error in a rounding error. Move a token amount and see if the sky fell. If nothing happened, move a little more. No one had ever touched the account. Banks forgot. Systems aged. People retired. The world turned.

In his mind, he was smarter than the world. He had proven that once. He could prove it again. He made himself a rule: he would wait 90 days after Collins' sentencing. If by then nothing stirred, he would act. Not recklessly. Not greedily. Reasonably.

Ninety days passed like a slow train. On the 89th, he woke from a dream in which he typed the password to the account and found not numbers but a sentence: WE SEE YOU. He chuckled to himself in the bathroom with the water running and the fan on and told the mirror to grow up. On the 90th day, he walked around with the taste of metal under his tongue and avoided his laptop the way you avoid an old friend who knows too much.

On the 91st day, he came home early.

Bernice was at a neighbor's for coffee. The house was empty and clean, the afternoon light steeping the living room in that patient, honey-colored way that made everything look kinder than it was. He poured a glass of water and stared at the ice as if it would spell something.

He carried the laptop to the desk in the upstairs study and sat. He did not turn on the lamp. The screen woke and painted his face. He opened a blank text file first and typed the steps he would follow, the way he wrote a plan before a deployment: open secure shell, verify the balance, generate a burner email unique to the session, start a token transfer to an unrelated destination under a false name, monitor for movement.

His hands were surprisingly steady.

He reached for the external drive where the credentials lived.

"Mail," Bernice called from downstairs.

He jumped, heart slamming, then laughed at himself.

"Up here," he said, voice working its way back from the bottom of a pit.

He heard the door, the soft thud of it closing with her hip, the slap of envelopes on the hall table.

She started up the stairs.

"Forwarded stuff," she said at the landing, lifting a rubber-banded bundle. "Must've been a mix-up at the post office. Los Angeles?" She made a face. "Who do we know in LA?"

Matt turned the drive in his fingers until the bottom edge dug into his palm. "Probably junk," he said lightly.

Bernice peeled a plain brown envelope from the front of the bundle and handed it to him. A month-old postmark was there, with a forwarding label slanted at the corner, and another on top. The return address was a PO box. The weight was nothing.

He slid a finger under the flap and opened it.

Inside was a single sheet of thin paper—Commonwealth Trust Bank of Antigua. The letterhead looked cheaper than he remembered.

Dear Sir or Madam,

As required by applicable banking and anti-money laundering regulations, including enhanced procedures mandated by post-9/11 US and international AML laws, we are conducting an internal review of certain dormant and/or inactive accounts for which beneficial ownership cannot be verified.

Our records show an account in the name of Square Consulting LLC, which has been inactive for some time. Our attempts to contact the registered officers at the last known address have been unsuccessful.

As part of our review and in advance of potential regulatory reporting, we request documentation establishing current beneficial ownership and source of funds. If we do not receive satisfactory information within thirty (30) days of this notice, we may be required to restrict the account, report the matter to relevant authorities, and take such other actions as our policies and applicable law require.

Please contact the Compliance Department at the number below.

Sincerely,
   Compliance Office
   Commonwealth Trust Bank of Antigua

The paper blurred. He blinked, and it cleared. His chest felt too small for his lungs. The room had not changed, but it had tilted, just a degree, just enough to slide the glass of water across the desk without moving it.

Bernice was saying something about the neighbor's hydrangeas. He could hear her voice but could not hear the words. He folded the letter and opened it again, as if he could will it to change.

"Anything we need to deal with?" she asked finally, leaning on the doorframe.

"Junk," he said, and smiled with his teeth.

She nodded slowly, not convinced, but unwilling to pry with the afternoon floating between errands. "I'm taking Mark to get new sneakers before dinner. You coming?"

"I'll catch up," he said. "Half an hour."

When she left, he read the letter again and again until the sentences were just shapes.

This was what he had wanted, wasn't it? To be forgotten?

To be so still that the account fell off the edge of the bank's memory and into the basement, where compliance interns kept lists.

He had given them a false address in Los Angeles to stop them from sending things to his house. The bank had sent the letter there dutifully, and the postal service had carried his lie back to him with a fluorescent sticker and a shrug.

Dormant and/or inactive accounts for which beneficial owner-ship cannot be verified.

He had made the account look exactly like that. He had made a hole in their records. And now the hole had a shape around it, a bright outline, a line item on a spreadsheet titled ACTION REQUIRED.

He put the letter down and stared at his hands. They remained steady. His mind had already begun to do what it always did: draw maps. If he waited, ignored the letter entirely, the bank might restrict the account. Restriction was not forfeited. Restriction was a door closed from the outside that someone could open with the right key. If he responded, if he called, what would he say? What could he safely say that would not brand his name to that number forever? Would attempting a transfer while the account was flagged trigger an endless alarm?

He pictured a room somewhere, with cool air, carpet that swallowed footsteps, and a row of monitors showing lists, where his account had just landed in a queue. He saw a junior analyst with a red pen and a manager who circled the largest balances for escalation, eventually sending a report to a regulator whose software searched for patterns with names like Collins and Summit and Goose.

He closed the laptop without meaning to and sat still.

Downstairs, he heard the front door open and close and the small sounds a house makes when people leave it: the settling of wood, the low hum of the refrigerator, the unresolved chords of his life.

On his desk, the external drive lay beside the letter, like a choice.

He thought of Derek Collins saying, "That number is not possible," and then staying completely silent.

He thought of the agents in his living room, their shoes neat on his rug, their questions polite, their eyes resting on him as if the story were a painting they were stepping closer to see.

He thought of Bernice in the doorway, a dish towel in her hands, trying to read him, trying to believe him.

He slid the external drive back into the desk drawer and closed it carefully.

He did nothing for a long time. The house held its breath with him.

Eventually, he stood, picked up the letter, and read it one last time. At the bottom was a direct line to the compliance office, and an email address that looked as though it hadn't been changed in years. He imagined how that inbox looked: a dozen real things drowned in a hundred spam messages about software licenses and toner.

He folded the page and slipped it into a manila folder marked TAXES, which he had not opened since April. Then, he put the folder on the highest shelf in the closet behind the coats that the kids wore only on holidays. He closed the closet door, opened it again, and moved the folder behind a shoebox, for good measure.

On his way down the stairs, his hand slid along the banister, feeling for splinters he knew weren't there. Smiling, he met Bernice and Mark on the walk, seeing the new sneakers. He told the neighbor that the hydrangeas looked great. He asked Stella about spelling and listened to Alfie recount the plot of a show as if it were a mission briefing.

After dinner, when the kids were in bed, he stood with Bernice at the kitchen sink, drying the last glass. "You're far away tonight," she whispered.

"Just tired," he said, and kissed her cheek.

In bed, he lay awake and stared at the ceiling until the ceiling stared back. He thought of how quiet everything had become after Collins went away, and of how loud a single sheet of paper could be.

Silence, he understood now, was never safety.

It was the loudest alarm of all, and it was ringing for him.

The next morning, he booked a family vacation for two weeks in Antigua.

ABOUT THE AUTHOR

D.P. Dart is an author of financial thrillers who spent over
thirty years in senior leadership
roles across global banks and
fintech companies.

His work in technology and
operations exposed him to the
inner workings of Wall Street,
the high pressure of corporate
boardrooms, and the gray areas
where ambition and morality
collide.

Retired in 2021, David now lives in Florida with his wife, where
he writes part-time. *Skim* is his second novel, following his
debut, *Planted*.

www.ingramcontent.com/pod-product-compliance
Lightning Source LLC
Chambersburg PA
CBHW022111240626
47153CB00007B/2328